A Treasury of Australian Folklore

A TREASURY OF AUSTRALIAN FOLKLORE

BILL BEATTY

Published for
Lifetime Distributors
6/8 Victoria Avenue, Castle Hill, New South Wales, 2154

by
Murray Child & Company Pty Ltd
64 Suffolk Avenue, Collaroy, New South Wales, 2097
Edited by Carolyn Child
Cover design by Emma Seymour
Text design by Murray Child
© The Estate of the late Bill Beatty
Printed by Australian Print Group, Maryborough, Victoria

National Library of Australia Catalogue Card No. and ISBN
1 86436 014 3

Cover illustration: Tom Roberts, Australia, 1856–1931,
Bailed up, 1895–1927, oil on canvas, 134.5 x 182.8 cm,
Art Gallery of New South Wales, Purchased 1933

The line illustrations used throughout this book
were reproduced from engravings in
Cassell's Picturesque Australasia, edited by E. E. Morris, 1889 and
Australasia Illustrated, edited by Andrew Garran, 1892.

CONTENTS

Author's Foreword
TO THE FIRST EDITION

The term 'Australian folklore' may surprise some people. There are many who have the erroneous idea that we have not had sufficient time in our short history to develop folk-lore which is usually the process of centuries.

What forms of traditional knowledge do we possess handed down amongst the ordinary people? Have we anonymous songs and sayings, stories and legends accepted by the people, describing their way of life and expressing their ideas and sentiments? We certainly have.

True, we can boast of few traditional folk dances; they embrace only a small selection of bush dances such as the 'Stockyards Quadrille' and the 'Bushmen's Scottische'. Women were scarce in early Australian communities, so there was little chance for development of much native dance form. So, too, there was little originality shown in music. Barely half of early Australian songs and ballads have native tunes, most of them being sung to traditional airs of the British Isles.

Romance was not entirely absent in this masculine world, as witness the ballad 'The Banks of the Condamine'—the story in song of the loving Nancy pleading to her shearer sweetheart to be allowed to go with him:

> *Oh, Willie dearest Willie, I'll go along with you,*
> *I'll cut off all my auburn fringe and be a shearer, too.*
> *I'll cook and count your tally, love, while ringer-o you shine,*
> *And I'll wash your greasy moleskins on the banks of the Condamine.*

In his *Dictionary of Australian Slang* Sidney J. Baker has revealed the astonishing extent of vernacular word-coinage developed in the brief period of white settlement in this country. We have an abundance, too, of tall tales and highly exaggerated mythical characters, but these humorous yarns I have omitted from this volume except where they are incorporated into a ballad such as that delightfully droll ditty 'The Old Bark Hut' with its fabulously large flies and fleas:

> *Faith, such flocks of fleas you never saw, they are so plum and fat*
> *And if you make a grab at one he'll spit just like a cat.*
> *Last night they got my pack of cards, and were fighting for the cut —*
> *I thought the devil had me in the old bark hut.*

In preference to the inclusion of some of the countless tall tales such as those about the size of Queensland stations where the shearer's cook has to go out in a boat to stir the soup, and so forth, I have chosen those which appear to be authentic. One such instance concerns a consignment of six tons of mustard going forward to a particular station in central-western Queensland, though the order was the result of error rather than design. The large pastoral agency in the south queried the item reading '6 tons mustard' on the squatter's order and sought enlightenment in a telegram suggesting that six tins was meant. The squatter replied testily that he knew what he was doing when it came to ordering six months supplies for the station, and he did not want any jackanapes counter-jumper in the city telling him his business. So the six tons of mustard was forwarded by ship, rail and bullock team. The tanks in which it was shipped are still rusting on one block of the property—a monument to a pioneer's pig-headedness.

The collecting of this roundup of folklore and forgotten or dimly remembered tales has occupied many years. It all began in my youth when I spent a holiday at a convict-built farmhouse in the Kurrajong district of New South Wales. The elderly owner often regaled me with stories which his father had told him concerning the early days. One of these tales fired my ambition to rescue such material from oblivion and to put it on record.

Covering almost the entire field of our popular history, my task has been a relentless but rewarding pursuit. I am indebted to other writers who have recorded the Australian story and to many people in town and country for their personal and textual help in providing material. Some sections of the book have served as the basis for articles for newspapers, magazines and radio programmes.

Documentary evidence has been given wherever possible, but in many cases it is impossible to confirm stories and happenings which are merely heresay and undoubtedly embellished and embroidered down the years. All one can do is to endeavour to capture the story as recalled by old-timers. It has ever been thus with folklore, no matter what the country. Historians and scientists may try to discredit such tales but they will always be part of the native product. It does not matter whether or not King Alfred burnt the cakes or George Washington chopped down the cherry tree. What matters is that the English still have a lingering belief that a monarch may be scolded, and the Americans that one cannot, in conscience, tell a lie.

In a foreword to *Come A-Waltzing Matilda* I said that the book was a selection from a more extensive compilation of Australian folk-lore and forgotten tales I had gathered over the years, and which, I hoped, would eventually be published in full. My ambition is now realised, and I am happy to have the privilege of being able to put this material on record.

BILL BEATTY, 1960

vii

Publisher's Note

Bill Beatty was a popular journalist, author, naturalist and broadcaster during the 1950s and 1960s. His knowledge of Australiana was boundless and before his death over twenty years ago he had a fascinating and entertaining way of portraying it in print.

From the rich collection of material gathered from his many journeys around the Australian continenent, he wrote twelve absorbing and informative books, many of which were translated and published in Europe. *A Treasury of Australian Folklore* was first published in 1966 and was reprinted numbers of times but by the mid-1970s it had sadly disappeared from the shelves and until recently was almost forgotten. Ernestine Hill wrote of him 'I have followed with admiration the work of Bill Beatty for many years. His perception of matters of universal interest, the lively imagination and dramatic quality he lends to the leaf of a tree or an aboriginal legend, a convict mutiny or a coral reef, have won for him a unique place among our writers of Australia with a zest of brevity and humour that appeals to everyone…'

The stories in this book are as fresh and interesting today as the day they were written. Bill Beatty captured the very essence of the early days of Australia and the passage of time since he wrote these stories, far from dulling their focus has probably sharpened it; the reader is intimately involved with everyday events of the last two centuries, witnessing gold robberies, shipwrecks, mining disasters and all manner of dramatic and tragic occurrences which would be fascinating enough if fiction but positively riveting when seen as fact.

I am pleased to be able to bring the work of this fine writer to a new generation of readers and am confident that it will find a permanent place in the folk literature of our country.

MURRAY CHILD

ONCE A JOLLY SWAGMAN

Origin of 'Waltzing Matilda'; Swaggie Joe and Matilda; Banjo Paterson and Christina McPherson; The swagman; Swagmen's Unions; Christina McPherson and bushranger Morgan.

If you asked almost any non-Australian what is Australia's national song, the chances are that he would reply, 'Waltzing Matilda'. This ballad with its haunting tune and homely words is known wherever Australians are found—and that covers practically the whole wide world.

Many versions are given of the origin of the term, 'Waltzing

WALTZING MATILDA
BY A. B. PATERSON

Once a jolly swagman camped beside a billabong,
*   Under the shade of a coolibah tree,*
And he sang as he sat and waited while his billy boiled,
*   'Who'll come a-waltzing Matilda with me—*
Waltzing Matilda, waltzing Matilda, who'll come a-waltzing
*   Matilda with me?'*
And he sang as he sat and waited while his billy boiled,
*   'Who'll come a-waltzing Matilda with me?'*

Down came a jumbuck to drink at the billabong
*   Up jumped the swagman and grabbed him with glee,*
And he sang, as he stowed it away in his tucker-bag,
*   'Who'll come a-waltzing Matilda with me?*
Waltzing Matilda, waltzing Matilda, who'll come a-waltzing
*   Matilda with me?'*
And he sang as he stowed it away in his tucker-bag,
*   'Who'll come a-waltzing Matilda with me?'*

Up came the squatter, riding on his thoroughbred,
*   Down came the troopers—one, two, three—*
'Whose is the jumbuck, you've got in your tucker-bag?
*   You'll come a-waltzing Matilda with me.*
Waltzing Matilda, waltzing Matilda, who'll come a-waltzing
*   Matilda with me?*
Whose is the jumbuck you've got in your tucker-bag.
*   You'll come a-waltzing Matilda with me.'*

Up jumped the swagman, and sprang into the billabong,
*   'You'll never take me alive!' said he.*
And his ghost can be heard, as we pass beside the billabong,
*   'Who'll come a-waltzing Matilda with me?*
Waltzing Matilda, waltzing Matilda,
*   Who'll come a-waltzing Matilda with me?'*
And his ghost can be heard as we pass beside the billabong,
*   'Who'll come a-waltzing Matilda with me?'*

Matilda'; there are also many accounts of the inspiration for the words and the source of the tune. The most authentic story concerning the term seems to come from East Gippsland, Victoria. This is handed down as a folk tale among the settlers in that district of tall timbers.

Matilda is said to have been the first woman swaggie to be seen in Victoria. She and her husband, Joe, were very well known and respected throughout East Gippsland; their surname was unknown, and the wife was always called Mrs Swaggie Joe. Matilda and Joe were entirely happy in their carefree life, wandering the old bush tracks winter and summer, Joe with his bluey on his back, Matilda with a smaller swag on hers.

Matilda often told how her father reacted when Joe asked him for his daughter's hand:

'What! My daughter marry a common swaggie? A man who can't offer her even a shack to live in! Do you think I'd let you go a-waltzing Matilda all over the countryside?'

Despite this opposition the girl married Joe and set off with him on a lifetime of wandering through the spacious countryside, which they understood and loved from the bottom of their hearts.

Eventually the day came when they grew infirm, their youthful strength and vigour sapped by the years. They were offered a home by a kindly couple living at Bruthen, but they refused it, saying that they could never live indoors like other folks, and they would go on until they came to the end of the track.

Then one sad day Matilda was taken ill in the morning and died at midday. Swaggie Joe dug her grave at the foot of an old gum tree and sat with his arms about her until it grew dark. Then he buried her.

Next morning as he prepared to fasten on his bluey he muttered, 'Oh well, Bluey, you'll have to be Matilda to me now, and we'll waltz along together 'til the end.'

Swaggie Joe's name for his bluey was soon adopted by other sundowners. 'Waltzing the bluey' was already their idiom for tramping with their swag, so it was not long before it evolved into 'Waltzing Matilda'. It is said that Joe developed the habit of talking to his swag when alone in the bush. He was sometimes seen with it propped against a tree while he talked to it, addressing it as 'Matilda'.

Now for the origin of the words and tune of the song. The verses were written by the Australian poet, A. B. ('Banjo') Paterson in 1896, when he was staying at the home of his fiancee, Miss Sarah Riley, at Winton, Queensland. One day they visited Mr Robert McPherson, owner of Dagworth, one of the largest sheep stations in the district. McPherson and his sister, Christina, were driving Paterson and Miss Riley home when, in a paddock, they saw an old swagman trying to catch a sheep for his tuckerbox. McPherson stopped the buggy, exclaiming, 'He's after a jumbuck!' And jumping down he chased the swaggie away. (Jumbuck was the name coined for a sheep by the Aborigines.)

This incident caught Paterson's imagination and he softly spoke the first lines of 'Waltzing Matilda'.

Miss McPherson was intrigued with the words and told the poet that some time previously she had heard a brass band playing a tune that she thought would suit them. When they reached Miss Riley's home Paterson and Miss McPherson sat down at the harmonium and adapted the tune to the words. The tune is an old Rochester (Kent) marching air of the Marlborough Wars. In 1903 Marie Cowan set the music in its present arrangement.

Incidentally, as a baby, Christina McPherson, who was responsible for the music of 'Waltzing Matilda', figured in the capture of Daniel Morgan.

When that bushranger held up the McPherson homestead, then at Peechelba, Victoria, he ordered food to be brought to him while he kept the family in range of his gun. Then he 'requested' Mrs McPherson to play the harmonium to him while he ate. As the baby, Christina, kept crying in the next room, he angrily told a maid to 'go out and keep that brat quiet'.

The maid did so, but having calmed the child, she climbed through the window, raced to an adjoining property, gave the alarm, came back through the window and walked into the main room as though nothing had happened. As a result Morgan was captured. In endeavouring to escape he was shot dead by a station hand.

The Australian swagman must not be confused with the hobo of America or the English tramp. These latter two classes consisted mainly of vagrants who subsisted by begging, stealing or living off the country, and had no intention of working if it could be avoided.

The Australian swagman was the product of conditions in the days of expanding settlement. A continent was being developed and, in fertile areas, farming was being added to sheep grazing on large holdings of pastoralists, who were known as squatters, because in the early days of settlement large areas of land were secured by 'squatting rights'. Labour was a fluid force following seasonal needs to a large extent.

Sheep shearing began in Queensland about July and the shearers followed the job southward for over a thousand miles as spring spread down through New South Wales and Victoria. Each man made his own way from 'shed to shed', as the jobs were called.

Railways were non-existent in the back country, so the sundowner, or swagman, evolved a minimum pack of his necessities and went 'waltzing his bluey' along the track. 'Waltzing' came from the habit of some of the swagmen of moving round a circle of stations, generally completing the journey in about six months. The route he travelled was called 'the racecourse'.

At the sheep stations he could draw free rations of tea, sugar and flour as a traveller passing through. This issue was not regarded as a charity, but partly as a means of maintaining a mobile force of labour and partly in recognition of the vast distances between settlements and normal supply sources.

The swagman was usually a versatile worker, skilled in the rural handicrafts which were the daily portion of the pioneer. If not shearing he might be harvesting grain, picking fruit, building fences, sinking dams or clearing scrub, often on a contract basis rather than wages. Many of the swaggies were young men taking a look at the country; they covered thousands of miles before deciding on a bit of land to start on their own account. Meanwhile they banked the proceeds of their various contracts.

Some of the older men loved the free, wandering life and merely accumulated enough money for a spell of gregarious conviviality at some bush pub. When the cash was done they took their headaches and a last bottle of firewater back on the 'wallaby track'.

When a man took to the track he was 'on the wallaby', because a wallaby makes many small tracks through the bush. His swag was his 'bluey', so called after the grey-blue blanket which was always rolled round the outside; it is not very often seen nowadays.

The Swagmen's Union

Maybe it was an example of typical bush humour but according to old residents of Forbes, New South Wales, a union of swagmen was once formed on the banks of the Lachlan River. It seems that the meeting was largely attended by the best tucker cadgers in the country. Officers were elected and the following rules drawn up:

1. No member to be over one hundred years of age.
2. Each member to pay one pannikin of flour entrance fee. Members who don't care about paying will be admitted free.
3. No member to carry swags weighing over 10 pounds [4.5 kilograms].
4. Each member to possess three complete sets of tucker-bags, each set to consist of nine bags.

5. No member to pass any station, farm, boundary rider's hut, camp or homestead without tapping and obtaining rations or handouts.
6. No member to allow himself to be bitten by a sheep. If a sheep bites a member he must immediately turn it into mutton.
7. Members who defame a 'good' cook, or pay a fine when run in, shall be expelled from the union.
8. No member is allowed to solicit baking-powder, tea, flour, sugar or tobacco from a fellow unionist.
9. Any member found without at least two sets of bags filled with tucker will be fined.
10. No member to look for or accept work of any description. Members found working will be expelled.
11. No member to walk more than 5 miles [8 kilometres] per day if rations can be obtained.
12. No member to tramp on Sunday at any price.

Arrival organisation was the Bagmen's Union of Australia. Its self-appointed president was a man named Kemp. There were no other office-bearers, the head office being just wherever the president happened to be camped. Kemp had a book of rules printed which stipulated the regulations for accepting tucker, lifts on the road, opening and shutting of gates, treatment of dogs, sharing fires, correct method of carrying swags and billycans. A member was allowed to have two straps on his swag, but after five years on the track he was entitled to add a third strap which elevated him to the rank of sergeant.

BUSH CHARACTERS AND BUSH CUSTOMS

Bush Characters; Shinplasters; The Stockwhip; Emu as a Weather Prophet; Of Bush Origin; Damper; Bush Initiative; Customs and Traditions.

BUSH CHARACTERS

Gone are the swagmen of yesterday and with them has gone most of the colour associated with carrying the swag.

'Hollow-log Jack' frequented the Monaro country. He reckoned he never slept anywhere but in a hollow log, and swore that there wasn't a camping-place to equal it. He knew every hollow log along the routes he travelled and cleaned out many of them. When he moved on he plugged the ends so that snakes and rabbits would not take possession. According to Hollow-log Jack a man needed only one blanket on the very coldest of nights in these bunks. One end was plugged to stop draughts. Sometimes he walked late into the night to reach a log. His dog went in first and cleared out any wild intruders; then the dog crawled out and the swagman crawled in. Appropriately enough, Jack was found dead in a hollow log.

'Doggy Tom' was known to every man and woman on the south coast of New South Wales. He always had at least a dozen dogs with him, and he camped with them at night and tramped the roads with them by day. Doggy Tom was found dead one day with his dogs guarding his body.

Some of the sundowners used to sow pumpkin, marrow, melon and other seeds near camping-places to ensure supplies of vegetables when they worked round that way months afterwards. 'Pumpkin Paddy' had over one hundred such gardens around the Condamine and Warrego Rivers. He liked potatoes and carried small ones, and thick peel, in a billy for sowing.

Lemon-trees growing in unexpected places along the Richmond River are known as the Parson's Lemons after the Reverend A. C. Selwyn, who used to ride on horseback to stations and selections, carrying pocketfuls of citrus seeds to be sown by the river as 'comfort for future travellers'.

'Quandong Joe' was known all over the west of New South Wales. He had quandong seeds on his clothes for buttons, and quandong seeds suspended from his hat to keep the flies from his face. From these seeds he made necklaces, rosary beads, and all kinds of novelties. He also made jam from quandongs and invariably feted a visitor to his camp with one of his quandong pies, in which he specialised.

'Charcoal Annie' was a woman sundowner in the Riverina district who burnt charcoal in river bends and sold it to blacksmiths. She seemed always middle-aged, always carried a sack on her back, and had great, deep, haunted eyes. She lived alone, did no wrong, and died a mystery.

'Billy Patches', a Queensland character, was so-called because of the many neat patches on his clothes. On his death a banknote was found sewn under each patch.

'Old Bob' deserves inclusion in any list of bush characters. He was a boundary-rider who spent most of his spare time with paints and brushes. In any picture he painted it was a certainty that there would be a fence of some sort. Old Bob had a mania for painting fences, whether his picture was of a horse, cow, hut or cottage. He had pictures of such fences as the dog-leg, chock-and-block, post-and-rail, the lazy cocky's, and those varied bush fences that are nameless. A collection of Old Bob's paintings would surely be a complete record of all the types of fences that have been erected in outback Australia.

'Nangus Jack' was a famous whip-maker. His whips were used all over the country. He would spend a week or two making whips for any station he visited; stockwhip, buggy whip, and other kinds. The job finished, he would move on to another station. If things were slack he plaited whips and took them to saddlers in the townships, where they were sold for him. He never turned out a shoddy article. Everything he plaited was a first-class job. When not making whips he plaited bridles, halters, belts, braces and leather watch-chains. Nangus Jack was found dead on Old Man Plains, between Hay and Deniliquin, with one of his whips in his hand, as he would have wished to pass on.

One of the queerest characters ever to roam the outback was Paddy Lenny, known as 'The Horse King of the Northern Territory'. Although he did not own one acre of country, Lenny had at one time over eight hundred horses. With the assistance of a couple of native boys he used to travel his horses from one waterhole to another seeking the best feed. Threats by irate station managers never worried Lenny, and though he hardly ever had enough to eat in his camp, the old Horse King refused to sell one of his horses. Upon his death in Darwin, the Public Curator employed stockmen to muster Lenny's horses so that they could be sold, but drovers and others in the Territory had got in early, as soon as they heard of his death, and purloined many of the animals. One year a buyer offered Lenny £8 a head for all the horses he could muster—at that time he had nearly seven hundred—but the old fellow refused. He preferred to keep his horses and roam the Territory in poverty.

A picturesque character was a woman known all over western Queensland as 'Red Jack'. Her real name was Annie Doyle. For more than twenty years she wandered the west, never remaining long in any locality. Red Jack was a rough character, a slim, wiry woman crowned with a thatch of long red hair, usually bundled up and sometimes skewered with a stick. She dossed at a campfire like the ordinary battler on the road, and knew the wide spaces better than most men. She was a first-class drover, but would tackle any kind of work at a pinch. Dressed like a man on the overland, and with her fiery locks under a wide-brimmed hat, she passed easily for a man and was always addressed as Jack. She owned two smart horses, riding one and leading the other. With these horses she attended every bush race meeting, training them and riding them in the various events. Her most memorable race was at Cloncurry, a match for £10 with a Chinese, who thought he owned the champion of the west. The race—a mile—was held on a Sunday, and all Cloncurry turned out to see it. The Chinese was a splendid rider, but he lacked Annie's experience. After a desperate neck and neck race in which the celestial's pigtail came down and Red Jack's bundle of hair followed suit, Annie won by half a head. Her racings and her wanderings ended at Mareeba, North Queensland, where she died in 1902.

SHINPLASTERS

Currency theorists may be interested in a practice which, for good or ill, has fallen into disuse. At one time printed notes of various denominations were issued by storekeepers over most of north-west Queensland. They could be cashed anywhere in that vast area just the same as banknotes. They were nicknamed 'shinplasters'. As might be expected, there was a certain amount of abuse. Although forgeries were uncommon, there was another way by which the public could be cheated. Unscrupulous storekeepers issuing these notes would often bake them in a hot oven and slightly dampen them. As a result, after a certain period, they would crumble to bits. Many a bushman taking change in these notes would find on arrival at another town that the shinplasters had turned into powder and were utterly useless.

The Stockwhip

And he raced his stockhorse past them
And he made the ranges ring
With the stockwhip, as he met them face to face.

'Banjo' Paterson's song of the stockwhip recalls the fact that the stockwhip is a symbol of the Australian outback; the constant companion of the stockman who handles cattle, wild horses and sheep.

The Australian stockman rides a different kind of horse, wears different clothes, uses different gear from men who handle stock in other parts of the world. One of the things that sets him apart is his stockwhip. Like him it is unique. What the lariat is to the North American cowboy, the bolas to the South American gaucho, and the zhambok is to the South African, the whip is to the Australian stockman. When a whip is used in other countries it is short-handled and made for striking rather than cracking.

Australian whips have been sent all over the world, but mainly as curiosities, for it takes an Australian stockman to handle them. A whip plaited by an expert is a beautiful piece of work. It is really two whips— one is plaited and another plaited over the top of the first. Eight feet (2.5 metres) is the average length of the stockwhip, though some are made up to 20 feet long (6 metres). 'Saltbush' Bill Mills—one of the first bushmen to win international fame for his prowess with the stockwhip—used a 55-foot (17-metre) whip.

Kangaroo hide is the main reason why Australian whips are so good. For its weight it is much stronger than any other hide, and it works up into a fine finish. Plaited leather is used on the handle, which is just as important as the rest of the whip. A handle too long or too short can destroy the balance of the whip. The handle, and the way the whip is fixed by an interlocking keeper to the handle, is where the Australian whip differs most from others.

A man who uses a stockwhip all day becomes extremely accurate with it. No wonder it is called the stockman's 'third arm'. Cattlemen have been known to cut a brand on a beast's hide with a whip. Some of the fancy and trick cracks of the experts are remarkable. They can, to all appearances, flog a man unmercifully, yet they are not hurting him in the least, for they crack the whip about a foot (30 centimetres) to the side of the body and let it curl around harmlessly.

The Emu as a Weather Prophet

If you have ever tasted a cake made with an emu egg you will really know the meaning of the word 'rich'. One emu egg is equal to twelve hen eggs, and a cake made with one is just food for the gods. They are delicious, too, scrambled. But if you like your eggs boiled you must cook them for nearly half an hour and keep turning them in the water.

Many and varied are the methods adopted by bushmen to tell if the eggs are fresh. Emu eggs will keep fresh for nine months, or more, and if you smear some fat or wax over them they will last for years. To test their freshness bushmen often use the spinning method. You take three eggs and place them end to end on top of each other, holding the top and bottom ones in each hand. The pressure holds the egg in the centre. That centre egg, if it is fresh, will start to spin round and round. If it stays still, you will know it has had its day.

A medium-sized egg weighs about 1½ lb (680 grams). If a horseman comes across a nest, and has no means of carrying them, he usually takes off his shirt, ties the ends of the sleeves and fills the latter with the eggs. Then he puts a sleeve on each side of his saddle and rides home.

Outback folks regard the emu as an excellent weather prophet. The birds will lay their eggs only if they know there will be rain soon, with plenty of juicy green feed for the chicks when they hatch out. If eggs are not found in the months when the birds usually lay, a dry season is indicated.

OF BUSH ORIGIN

The name 'billy' seems to be a purely Australian word. Legend says that it was first used in Western Australia on the goldfields.

In the early days France used to export quantities of tinned meat to the miners there. It was labelled 'Boeuf Bouilli' (boiled beef). As cooking utensils were extremely scarce on the goldfields the miners put the empty tins to good use. Some they used as drinking cups, others they put handles on to make pots for boiling water and cooking purposes. They called them 'bouilli' cans. It was only a matter of time before the name became billy can and was later shortened to billy.

The billy was one of the most widely used articles in outdoor Australia, popular among rich and poor alike. Swagmen sometimes carried sets of billies of graduated size that fitted inside each other. Rarely would you see a swaggie with a new or bright-looking billy. It branded him as a new chum, so he blackened it as quickly as possible, boiling it over smoky fires until it became a 'respectable' black.

Years ago, billy-boiling contests were popular pastimes at bush carnivals, especially in the districts where drovers used to meet. Some of the entrants carried special billies for these contests. They were as thin as tissue paper. No black or soot stained them, for the cleaner the billy the quicker it boils. Also the fire needs to be a small, compact one, kept directly under the billy.

From Western Australia also came the invention of the Coolgardie safe. It was on the goldfields, too, that this had its origin. Ice was unknown in those parts, but the miners soon solved the problem of keeping food cool and fresh with this safe. The principle was sound but simple. A tray of water on the top of the food container was connected with a drip tray underneath, by means of strips of hessian. The water kept the hessian sides damp, and, as the safe was placed in a current of air, the process of evaporation lowered the temperature inside the safe. It was only necessary to keep water in the top tray in order to maintain food in the safe cool and fresh.

From somewhere in the outback came the idea of the tuckerbox. Every bushman who travelled in any kind of vehicle carried a box as a food receptacle. An ideal one was made from a gin case. Small holes were cut in the ends, and these were covered with fine gauze wire to allow air to circulate in the tucker-box, and also to keep out the flies. Whilst the food was being eaten in front of the camp-fire the tucker-box served as a seat.

Apart from the invention of such makeshift masterpieces as the Murrumbidgee blanket and the Wagga rug, it is claimed that the wire mattress was the invention of an Australian bushman. The Wagga rug is made from old sacks. The Murrumbidgee blanket is also made from old sacks with the addition of strips of paper-bark sewn inside it. The first bush wire mattress was merely a frame of saplings. Holes were bored into the wood so that fencing-wire could be interlaced to form a platform on which gum leaves or dry grass were placed. It formed a snug and comfortable bed. Later on netting wire was substituted for the fencing-wire. It is said that the first bush telephone was invented in the early 1890s by Edward Argyle, manager of Gunbower sheep station, Victoria. He bought at a Melbourne shop a toy-like telephone gadget, which he tried out to practical use on his fence. To his surprise it worked, and it was not long before the fences were wired to communicate with outlying stations. The scheme was widely adopted, not only in Australia, but on the ranches of Texas and Arizona. American papers, including the *Scientific American*, published the story of the Australian origin of the outback 'phone service.

DAMPER

Most people take it for granted that Australian damper originated in the bush. According to the historian Bonwick, the inventor was a First Fleeter named William Bond, Australia's first baker, who had his place of business in Pitt Street, Sydney. This pioneer died in 1838, at the reputed age of a hundred and ten.

Probably through lack of facilities for making the common bread loaf, much of the bread he made at first was 'damper'.

The name 'damper' was derived from his custom of 'damping' the fire—covering it with ashes, so as to preserve the red coals with which

to make a blaze in the morning. The bush damper is still covered in much the same manner.

When the pioneers trail-blazed the bush there were no self-raising flours, baking-powders or yeast. Nevertheless, bushmen and women had many substitutes for baking-powder, the most popular being a handful of white wood-ashes. In the artesian bore country, bore-water was sufficient to make the damper rise.

Damper always retained its popularity with swagmen. At Christmas time, when these wandering gentlemen foregathered in celebration, they sometimes put threepenny-bits in the damper!

The man outback seldom had a pair of scales, and even if he had a foot-rule he rarely used it. He measured corn, bran or anything else on his farm, with a kerosene-tin, and he was generally pretty accurate. By looking at a beast for a few moments he could judge within a pound or two its correct weight, and guessing the weight of a bullock is still popular at country shows. Timber could be measured with the hands. Bushmen knew exactly the width of their hands, how far they could span, and how many steps they took to a hundred yards. On the south coast of New South Wales a story is told of a woman who was famed for always winning the 'stepping the hundred yards' event at all country sports carnivals. However, an event at Wyndham was the last one she won. Just before she finished stepping the hundred yards (91 metres) a dog ran in front of her and she tripped and fell. Her dress flew up and revealed a piece of cord fastened from one leg to another so that by stepping the full extent of this cord she was able to measure her paces exactly.

Children of the great outback rarely saw sweets, and they knew nothing of cinemas and radio, but they made their own fun and entertainment. They roasted cobs of young corn at the fire, baked potatoes, quinces and apples in the hot ashes, gathered bunya-nuts and roasted them like chestnuts, used quandong seeds for marbles, after eating the fruit, and where bush-nuts were plentiful up north they had no need to buy peanuts. They used to eat the thick red mass from briar pips before experts knew it was rich in vitamin C. They made their own sporting material. Bush timber made cricket bats, and a fungus known as blackfellow's bread provided the balls. When dad killed a bullock they inflated the bladder and made a football. And then there were the joys of swimming in the creek, or billabong, or at least some kind of waterhole.

The prickly pear has been a costly menace to Australia, nevertheless it was a boon to the old-timers. Many have pulped the pear and used it as a cattle fodder with good results. Bush women have found that the fruit made delicious jam and jelly; indeed, where ordinary fruit was scarce many children have known no other jam. Bushmen in the outback, and sometimes children doing their homework for the correspondence schools, have written with prickly-pear juice as a substitute for ink. It has even been used as a paint. There are many people who swear by prickly pear as a remedy for diabetes. They boil some of the green leaves and drink the juice. And here's a tip regarding the spikes on the plant. They are an excellent substitute for gramophone needles, giving a mellow tone which is not obtainable from steel needles.

One of the most familiar bush utensils, especially during the summer months was the canvas waterbag. It was a boon to bush workers and rural travellers who were in need of a drink of cool water. The waterbag was introduced by Major Thomas Mitchell during his famous exploring expedition in south-western Queensland, in 1846. Mitchell had some trouble with the receptacles in which he had been carrying water. As an experiment he sewed pieces of canvas together to make a bag, which he greased with a generous supply of melted mutton tallow. Into the treated bag the Major poured some water and for the rest of the journey members of the party were never without a refreshing drink when needed. Previous to the introduction of the waterbag the old fashioned goat and sheep skin water containers were generally used by the pioneer settlers.

Many of the old bush habits and customs are fast dying out. The old bark hut has almost completely disappeared and with it the practice of hanging the frying pan outside the door after a man cooked his meal. The reason for this tradition is puzzling, as all other cooking utensils were kept inside. Invariably, outside the hut door, there was a wooden block on which the dweller sat in the evening. Alongside, there was usually a stout stick ready to deal with any snake that should disclose its presence. Trappers decorated the outside walls of their huts with wallaby and fox skins. As Christmas approached, the hind legs of a kangaroo or wallaby were hung up the chimney to smoke. These hams would be left for months and, when eventually cooked, made delicious eating.

Pit-sawing is almost a forgotten art, even in the far outback, though it was a vast improvement on the early pioneers' efforts at timber cutting. A pit was dug in a suitable timber location and a framework erected over it. The trees were cut and the logs sawn on the wide open framework over the pit. When the nearby timber had been used the whole outfit was moved to another stand. A man had to be a skilled tradesman to do good work with a pit-saw. There are still many bush homes of sawn slabs in splendid condition—some of them well over a century old—which were built with the aid of the pit-saw. A settler would dig his own pit and set up his saw, cutting all the timber for his home and furniture. You can still see a few old pits scattered about the bush country and they are often mistaken for deserted mining shafts.

In some little bush towns political meetings were made known by a man ringing a bell—usually the dinner bell from the local pub. At Wyndham, New South Wales, the priest used to borrow the dinner bell from the publican to call the people to Mass. It was used to announce also a visiting circus, a travelling picture-show or an auction.

Celebrating a wedding with 'tin kettling' was the recognised custom in many country districts. The local lads, armed with kerosene tins and lengths of doubled fencing wire, kept quiet until darkness enveloped the landscape. Then, the boys let themselves go! Those with tins hammered on them; those without tins showered handfuls of stones on the roof until the bridal couple asked them in to supper. But a local wedding was not considered successful until the couple were 'tin kettled'.

Shortage of tobacco and alcoholic beverages never worried the bushmen. Their pipes were generally hand-made, and of unusual design. Often they would dig up a piece of 'blackfellows' bread'—a kind of fungus found at the roots of eucalyptus trees—from which they would fashion a pipe. And they were good pipes, too, that gave a cool and comfortable smoke. To give the tobacco a better flavour they generally mixed an equal quantity of wild musk leaves with it. The tobacco would be kept in a snakeskin pouch.

Beer was made chiefly out of maize, and a good wine was made from blackberries. Many North Queensland bush dwellers made beer out of coconut-milk and brown sugar. A lot of these home-brews were exceedingly potent. At Glenrowan, Victoria, scene of the Kelly gang's last stand, a wine was made called 'Ned Kelly's Blood'. It was claimed to make one feel every bit as game as that gentleman of the road. Another heady beverage known as 'Drover's Ruin' was made from the fruit of the prickly pear.

To the pioneers, the cabbage-tree palm was surely the most useful plant growing in Australia. From the Aborigines they learned that the tender young hearts of the palm were good eating—they taste every bit as good as cabbage. Many a settler's home was thatched with the big leaves of the palm. Those roofs would last for many years, and they were completely waterproof. Housewives found that bundles of the leaves, bound together and fastened to a small sapling, made a splendid broom. And whole families would be seen wearing cabbage-tree hats. The men gathered bundles of the palm leaves and carried them home for their wives and children to plait into this most popular headgear.

There was plenty of work in the making of a cabbage-tree hat. The palm leaves were bleached, split into ribbons, and whilst still damp the strands were plaited and stitched into shape. For a hat band a bright silk puggaree was used, or maybe a band made of snakeskin or kangaroo leather. The hats for the womenfolk were silk lined and trimmed with handmade flowers. They were straw coloured, could be scrubbed and washed, and gave years of good service. They kept their shape, too, and were very cool. The cabbage-tree hat was the equal of any Panama and superior to most imported straw hats. After the famous Australian sculler, William Beach, won the world's sculling championship, his admirers presented him with a special one that was valued at twenty guineas. Other notable identities who favoured cabbage-tree hats were the poet Adam Lindsay Gordon and the novelist Marcus Clarke. Robert O'Hara Burke was wearing one when he set out from Melbourne on his tragic expedition across the continent.

There was a time when country hotels served purely Australian dishes. Wallaby-tail soup was often on the menu and, in the days before many of our native birds were protected, brush turkey, plain turkey and wonga pigeon. Kangaroo rissoles were always popular. At many little bush pubs satin-bird pie or parrot pie were firm favourites. Along the Murray River hotels served Murray River turtle soup. These fresh-water turtles were plentiful, and many good judges considered that the soup made from them was even better than the more famous turtle soup made from sea turtles. In the north-west of New South Wales and some parts of Queensland, wild goat meat was frequently on the menu, and while the wild goat is not a native of Australia, they were a pest in some parts and many preferred the flesh of a young goat to mutton. Galah was also a common enough dish in the north-west, but the galahs were pretty tough birds and not popular with travellers.* When hares were plentiful in the southern Monaro district, local hotels always served baked hare, and it was a favourite course. Rabbit was never popular on country hotel menus, possibly because they were regarded as a pest and also because so many rabbits suffered with hydatids (cysts, usually containing the lava of a variety of tapeworm).

Australians of the outback are noted for their extraordinary initiative, and not without good reason. They are masters of improvisation. Even when it comes to an everyday matter like correspondence their ingenuity is often astonishing, to say the least. Many a letter from isolated bush areas has been written with a wild turkey's quill dipped in the juice of an over-ripe prickly pear. Sometimes bush folk would strain the juice and bottle it, or just pick an over-ripe fruit when required and keep sticking the pen into it. All kinds of berries, too, have been used as substitutes for ink. Farmers in Gippsland used the juice of ripe blackberries, and even rabbits' blood! Paper, too, was often a problem for the dwellers of the backblocks. They wrote on the backs of jam tin labels and cigarette packets, and on brown paper that had been wrapped around parcels and even on sheets of paper bark.

*A sardonic bushman once gave me a recipe for cooking a galah: 'Put a stone in the bottom of the billy, then put in the galah and fill the billy with water. Boil until the stone is soft—then the galah will be cooked.'

One of the most unusual letters or cards that ever went through the post was sent by a bushman on the starched cuff of a dress shirt. He found the torn shirt on the road and having no writing paper ripped off a cuff, wrote on one side of it, and on the other side put the address and stuck a stamp on it. Another bushman wrote his letter on a thin sheet of dealboard with the address on the reverse side, affixing the stamp in the usual way. This also went through the post to its destination.

A central Queensland storekeeper has an odd collection of strange 'letters' from outback customers ordering various goods. One from an old prospector is scratched on the lid of a tobacco tin with a penknife. Then there is an order burnt on a piece of timber with a hot iron, and another written in pencil on both sides of a piece of pine from a kerosene case. But in no instance did any of these customers order writing material amongst their requirements!

Ordering goods from country storekeepers brings to mind the episode in which a bushman, tired of the plum jam that the local storekeeper had been sending for months, wrote in his next order: 'Two tins of jam—bar plum', meaning, of course, any other jam except plum. The storekeeper, however, read the order literally, and in a note sent with the goods he wrote: 'Sorry, I have no bar plum in stock, so am sending ordinary plum as usual.'

Perhaps one of the strangest addresses ever affixed to a letter was that of the settler who wrote to his wandering son 'C/- Conroy's Sheep along the Castlereagh'. The mailman, he reasoned, might easily miss a small post office, or be asleep as he passed it, but no one could possibly miss a flock of travelling sheep.

SOME AUSTRALIAN GHOSTS

Quinn's light; Fisher's Ghost; Ghost Glen; The Martinet Major; Black Horse of Sutton; Ghost of Glengallan Gates; Light that Fails— Ghost of Yarralumla; Morgan's Ghost; The Bunyip; Pony McQuinn's Waterhole; Tasmanian Ghosts; Devlin's Ghost; Murdering Sandhills; Ghosts of Cooper's Creek; Australia's Most Haunted House; The Guyra Ghost.

Australia's Ghosts seem to have died out in recent years. Perhaps the country has been opened up too much for them.

There were the Headless Horseman that caused cattle to stampede; the Tinonee ghost which appeared on a marshy flat near the Manning River; the Phantom Mail—a light which appeared to be on a mail-coach in the One Tree Plain district, near Hay, and which travelled rapidly across the plain. Men have galloped after it, but have never caught it.

Quinn's Light

No ghost can be altogether satisfactory unless it makes repeated and somewhat regular appearances. One spectre that endeavours to uphold a good ghostly tradition is Quinn's Light.

The strange phenomenon is well attested. It has chosen as its locale the Daudaman Valley in the Go-Go-Billi Ranges down by the Lachlan River, and it takes its name from one John Quinn, who for very many years was a judge at the New South Wales sheepdog trials and a man of sound common sense.

Quinn claimed that on numerous occasions he saw a strange light of extraordinary brilliance which came floating down the valley among the tall timbers, circled his homestead, then made back to its hills.

Quinn described it as resembling a large, yellow, crested eagle with outstretched wings, and said that it illuminated the trees as it passed with a phosphorescent glow. He showed it to others—in case his own testimony should not be believed—and he organised night riders who pursued it, and hunters who shot at the apparition but to no purpose.

Ghosts of the Glen

In the town of Kiama, on the South Coast of New South Wales, the old folks tell a ghostly tale of the early days there. The story is as old almost as the town itself.

The drama occurred in the days when ticket-of-leave men roamed the countryside—when Kiama was thickly timbered, and most of the men in the district were engaged in timbercutting.

Many an old resident could recall for you the vivid verse that tells of Kiama's blood-curdling ghosts

Over a pitfall, the moon dew is thawing,
And with never a body two shadows stand sawing,
The wraiths of two sawyers (step under and under),
Who did a foul murder, and were blackened with thunder;
And whenever a storm wind comes driving and driving,
Through the blood-spattered timber you may see the saw striving,
You may see the saw heaving and falling and heaving,
Whenever the sea-creek is chafing and grieving.

In the convict days many of the ticket-of-leave men were to be feared, especially those found amongst the Illawarra sawyers. They were a cut-throat crew who would stop at no evil deed.

One late night a young English immigrant, with a sheep-dog at his side, entered the inn at Kiama. He strolled over to the bar, calling out:

'Good evening, gentlemen! I'm a stranger to the district, but I hope you don't mind me joining the company. Have a drink, everybody! Come on—all of you! The drinks are on me!'

In 'shouting' for the crowd the young man foolishly displayed a purse full of money.

The evening passed, and then, slightly drunk, he decided to continue his journey.

Up spoke one of the few remaining drinkers: 'Now look here, new chum, me and me mate wouldn't think of letting you go out in the bush alone. Anyway, you'd never find your way on a pitch dark night like this. And, what's more, young feller-me-lad, if you're going south we can put you on the right track.'

And so the three men and the dog went into the darkness. They never returned.

It was some months later that a man well known in the district became lost in the thick bush near the present township of Gerringong. When night came he made a rough shelter in a glen and lay down and went to sleep. He awoke to the rumble of thunder. Suddenly he felt his eyes being drawn to an object a few yards away. To his horror he saw it was the doubled-up body of a man. A wasted sheep-dog was licking the dead face gashed, bloody and terrible to see.

Then he heard the rasping sound of a cross-cut saw and, looking farther into the darkness, he perceived the silhouetted figures of two men working in a saw-pit, complete with logs and crosspieces. A burst of thunder came and, as it died away, one of the men spoke:

'He's still got fifty golden sovereigns left. That's twenty-five apiece. A nice little nest-egg for us. We'll pitch the swine into the fire! But mind the dog—we'd better cut its throat.'

There was a flash of lightning and the apparition vanished.

Next day a search party found the lost man. He told his rescuers of the vision in the glen. Afterwards another search was made where the lost settler was discovered. At the spot he indicated, the burnt bones of a man were found—near by was the skeleton of a dog.

Years later, in the 1830s, a man walked into the same inn at Kiama. His name was Jem Hicks, and he had the drawn features of a haunted soul. Someone remarked that they hadn't seen him for a matter of years—in fact not since the time the new chum had 'shouted' for everyone and then disappeared.

All of a sudden a clap of thunder and lightning rent the air. A dog that was stretched out before the fire began to howl. Hicks started to tremble, and cried out:

'Curse the money! Curse the dog! Am I never to get peace?' In a stumbling rush he went into the night and was never seen again.

So ends the story of the ghosts of the glen. But not so the spectres themselves, for, as old-timers in the district will inform you, the ghostly tableau has appeared on several occasions to wanderers in the glen.

FISHER'S GHOST

Most historic of Australia's ghosts is Fisher's, at Campbelltown, New South Wales. Near Sydney, the road through Campbelltown, crosses a small creek on which is a neat sign marked Fisher's Ghost Creek

Of the thousands of motorists who have read that notice few have failed to wonder as to the origin of the name. Is there a story? There certainly is.

On the 17th of June, 1826 John Farley, a ticket-of-leave man, burst into the crowded parlour of the Plough Inn at Campbelltown. His face was pallid, his eyes staring, and he was shaking as if with the palsy. He cried out: 'A ghost! I've seen a ghost!'

An uproar of laughter greeted this dramatic announcement. Farley was bombarded from all sides by derisive questions and ribald inter-jections. The pub patrons agreed that he had been the victim of a practical joker, or else was suffering from hallucinations. But he stuck to his story.

'I was passing Fisher's farm and, as you know, there's a full moon outside. Leaning over the slip-rails I saw a man with a pipe in his mouth. But he wasn't smoking, and, when I got a bit nearer I saw it was Fred Fisher himself. Then I got panicky, for I could see right through him, as if he wasn't solid. I knew then that it wasn't Fred Fisher himself. It was his ghost!'

'How did you know it was Fred Fisher's ghost? How do you know he's dead?' someone called out.

True, Fred Fisher had simply disappeared from the district, and there had been no cause to believe other than that he'd gone elsewhere in the country.

'What was the ghost doing?' came another question.

Farley continued his story. 'He was just leaning over the sliprails. Then, as I went nearer, he began to point. I was too scared to move. Still, he kept on pointing down the paddock towards the creek. Then he just wasn't there—sort of faded away!'

Next morning Fisher's ghost was the one topic of conversation in the township. The news reached the local sergeant of police, who had already been making inquiries about Fisher's disappearance, and had notified the police headquarters in Sydney about the matter.

The sergeant decided to act on Farley's story. He sent a trooper and two native trackers to examine Fisher's property, remarking with a laugh not to expect to find footprints of a ghost.

No sooner had the party reached the slip-rails than Gilbert, one of the trackers, pointed to certain marks. There, smeared on the rails of the fence, in the exact position described by Farley, were traces of dried blood.

Soon, Gilbert gave a little cry of triumph. The whites of his eyes gleamed excitedly as he followed a trail towards the creek. There, at a particular spot, he directed the party to dig. In a few moments they came upon the body of Fisher dressed in the clothes described by Farley, and in the place he said the ghost had indicated.

Who was the murderer? Police investigations resulted in Fisher's partner, a man named Worrall, who was then living in Sydney, being charged with the crime. Though he protested his innocence he was found guilty and sentenced to death. On the day of his execution he confessed to the crime.

And to this day, in Campbelltown, the oldest inhabitants will tell you that if you care to wander, unaccompanied as did John Farley, round Fisher's farm about midnight on the night of the 17th of June you will see a dim figure leaning over the sliprails, pointing in the direction of the creek that runs at the bottom of the farm.

There is a sequel to this story. Mr J. K. Chisholm of Gledswood knew Farley well. When the latter was on his death-bed Mr. Chisholm went to see him. 'I want to ask you a question, Farley,' he said. 'Will you tell me the truth?'

Farley answered: 'I am a dying man, Mr Chisholm. I'll speak only the truth.'

'Well, it's only one question, Farley, and this is it: Did you really see Fisher's ghost, or did you make up that story because you had suspicions and wanted the matter investigated?'

Farley raised himself on his elbows painfully and looked straight at his visitor. 'Mr Chisholm, I saw that ghost as plainly as I see you now.'

Ghost of Glengallan Gates

This apparition was a gate opener in the Allora district of Queensland. Riders would feel their horses trembling and sweating with fear as they approached the gates. Then a grey, billowy form would fly from a post, and the gates would spring open. As soon as the horseman passed through, generally at a frenzied gallop, the gates would swing to again.

The haunting continued for many years, and seemed to defy explanation. Unbelievers claimed that the ghost was merely a large, whitish owl, which made the gate-post its nightly perch. When the bird rose at the approach of a horseman the sudden movement caused the finely-balanced gates to swing open, and then, having reached the limit of their movement, they swung back again.

The gates were removed some years ago, when the old track was transformed into a main road, but it is said that horses still betray terror when passing the crumbling gate stumps at night.

Records of the Monaro district of New South Wales abound in stories of wayside ghosts, shades of bushrangers who returned to the scenes of their crimes, sudden apparitions of the long since dead. Here are some picturesque tales of these spooks:

The Martinet Major

More than a century ago a certain major acquired large tracts of land in the Monaro district. A bachelor, he was a martinet of the worst kind. He had a number of convicts working for him, including an unruly member sent out as a political rebel. The latter resented the fact that he was 'a lag' along with the pickpockets and cut-throats working on the station and, as a result, always annoyed the peppery major.

One day the major abused this convict, who picked up a stone and threw it at him. The major, who was also a magistrate, immediately sentenced the man to death, and the hanging took place on the property that same evening.

But, so the story goes, the convict had his revenge. He haunted the place in a most annoying fashion, singing ribald songs at the foot of the major's four-poster bedstead; hunting the cattle out of the barns at night; kicking over buckets of milk left on the dairy floor by the milkmaids; rattling tins and tolling bells in the dead of night until the major could no longer stand it. Thoroughly exasperated, though he never admitted to being scared, he sold his property and returned to England.

BLACK HORSE OF SUTTON

Also in the Monaro district operated a famous spectre known as the Black Horse of Sutton. This apparition was seen at intervals by a certain family, but only when disaster befell their house. The first visitation took place when the father of the house went to Goulburn to arrange a land deal to extend his large property. As he was returning home he was thrown from his horse and killed.

It was a mild summer night and the man's wife was seated on the broad-flagged verandah of the homestead when she heard the faint echo of galloping hoofs along the dusty home road. There was silence; then the sound of a gate being opened; the wheeling of a horse as though a man had turned to close the gate; the clanging sound as it shut fast; then the sound of galloping hoofs again.

The woman stood up and walked to the top of the verandah steps to welcome her husband. . . .

'It must be John. Strange—I wonder why he didn't cooee as he always does? Why—I'm trembling! Perhaps it's just—oh! his horse! John! John! Where are you?'

A riderless horse had come into view, its hoofs drumming on the drive. It crossed the lawn at break-neck speed straight towards the house. The sound was muffled, only to be taken up again at the back of the house. The riderless horse had passed through the house and disappeared into the ranges beyond.

The woman watched it in the dusk petrified. She hoped it was a trick of her imagination in the fast-falling evening shadows. But she knew she would wait in vain for the return of her husband. When a search was made he was found dead his horse grazing near by.

Old identities in the district will tell you that when disaster came to that family the riderless horse was seen galloping swiftly—a messenger of death. It made its appearance when the woman's eldest son was killed at the Boer War. Again when the youngest son met his death in an accident.

The house has long been demolished and sheep graze across the country where the riderless horse comes no more.

BLACK GHOST OF YARRALUMLA

Yarralumla House, the beautiful Canberra residence of Australia's Governor-General, possesses a mystery of its own that is most intriguing. According to more or less conflicting versions of the story, a ghost—a real Australian black ghost—has been known to walk there.

The wanderer is popularly supposed to be an Aborigine searching for a lost diamond. But he is a very modest ghost who knows his place, never entering the house, but wandering about the lawns at Yarralumla, harmless and self-effacing.

It is said he has been seen from the dining-room on cold dreary nights when the breezes whistle down on Canberra from the snow-bound Monaro ranges.

On summer nights he has been seen digging under a deodar tree, where a diamond of great value, for which he is ever searching, is said to be hidden.

The tale is told in an unsigned manuscript dated 1881, 'written near Yarralumla'. The letter was found in this historic home after it had been handed over to the Commonwealth Government by its former owners. It states:

'In 1826, a large diamond was stolen from James Cobbity, on an obscure station in Queensland. The theft was traced to one of the convicts who had run away, probably to New South Wales. The convict was captured in 1858, but the diamond could not be traced; neither would the convict (name unknown) give any information, in spite of frequent floggings.

'During 1842 he left a statement to a groom, and a map of the hiding-place of the diamond.

'The groom, for a minor offence, was sent to Berrima gaol. He was clever with horses, and one day, when left to his duties, plaited a rope of straw and then escaped by throwing it over the wall, where he caught an iron bar. Passing it over, he swung himself down and escaped. He and his family lived out west for several years, according to the Rev James Hassall who, seeing him live honestly, did not think it necessary to inform against him. I have no reason to think he tried to sell the diamond. Probably the ownership of a thing so valuable would bring suspicion and lead to his re-arrest.

'After his death his son took possession of the jewel, and with a trusty blackfellow set off for Sydney. After leaving Cooma for Queanbeyan they met with, it was afterwards ascertained, a bushranging gang. The blackfellow and his companion became separated, and finally the former was captured and searched, to no avail, for he had swallowed the jewel.

'The gang, in anger, shot him. He was buried in a piece of land belonging to Colonel Gibbes, and later Mr Campbell. I believe the diamond to be among his bones. It is of great value. My hand is enfeebled with age, or I should describe the trouble through which I have passed. My life has been wasted, my money expended, I die almost destitute, and in sight of my goal.

'I believe the grave to be under the large deodar-tree. Being buried by blacks, it would be in a round hole.

'Believe and receive a fortune. Scoff and leave the jewel in its hiding-place.

'Written near Yarralumla.'

If the story is untrue, the deodar is not. The tree is considered to be the finest of its kind in the Commonwealth. No attempt has been made to uproot it, for the owners of Yarralumla have always thought more of this grand old tree than the chance of treasure among its roots, and they have left the jewel—if any—in its hiding-place. Many thousands of deodars growing throughout the country have been planted from the seeds of this famous old-timer with its absorbing tale of mystery.

Morgan's Ghost

Old hands around Woodend, Victoria, will tell you that the ghost of bushranger Dan Morgan still rides over the mountains in the vicinity at night. Not far from Woodend is Hanging Rock, claimed to be Morgan's hideout. There is an underground stream which emerges near the foot of the rock and runs over the cliff. The water in this stream is always rust coloured, and a deposit of red rust is left on the rocks. Because of this and the link with Morgan the water has long been referred to locally as 'Morgan's Blood.'

When Morgan was shot dead at Peechelba his head was cut off and sent to Melbourne to be examined for scientific purposes, which no doubt accounts for the story that the ghost riding about the hills is a headless ghost.

Behold the Bunyip

Mention of the bunyip will perhaps mean little to the present generation of young Australians. But there are many older folk who can vividly recall the fears inspired by lonely parts of the bush where they wandered as youngsters—fears arising from alleged association of the localities with this mysterious beast.

Despite some local variations, the story of the bunyip has so much in common throughout a considerable part of Australia that it is fair

to assume that the myth had a basis in some common act of natural history.

The bunyip of the Aborigines was a large, dark-coloured, furred animal, with glowing eyes and a bellowing call, a haunter of swamps and billabongs.

It did not take the white man long to get interested in the bunyip. Indicating a pre-knowledge, the first official reference appeared in the minutes of the Geographical Society of Australia, on the 19th December, 1821. The suggestion was recorded, following the report by the explorer Hamilton Hume of the existence of a strange animal in Lake Bathurst, supposedly a manatee, hippopotamus, or bunyip, that Hume be reimbursed for expenditure incurred in any further attempt to obtain hide, teeth or other tangible evidence of the existence of this creature.

In the early days of Victoria, before it became a separate colony, Governor Latrobe wrote that there were 'two kinds' of bunyip. He sent drawings of the 'southern' kind to Tasmania, but they were lost.

It may be that the 'northern' kind of bunyip was in part inspired by swamp-feeding cows, truants from the infant settlement of Parramatta. Early Sydney records of the marsh monster introduce horns and tasselled tails, which must have added special terror to the age-old stories of the local Aborigines. It is a pity that no copies remain of Latrobe's drawings of the bunyip. Contemporary Victorian writers called it the 'bunyip or kianpraty'.

There are records of alleged eyewitnesses. The year 1872 was the date of the Narrandera (New South Wales) bunyip, which was seen by many observers. It was described as: 'About half as long again as an ordinary retriever dog. Hair all over its body, jet black and shining. Its coat very long.' The following year one was recorded and described from Dalby, Queensland: 'It had a head like a seal, and a tail consisting of two fins, a larger and a smaller one.'

The Great Lake in Tasmania is supposed to have been inhabited by several bunyips. One bumped a boat in 1873. Francis McPartland, in 1870, saw three or four together. Seven observers in this locality, within ten years, all agree in describing the creature as like a huge sheep-dog about the head, and from three to five feet long.

There are many observers who steadfastly believe, and with much reason, that the actual origin of the widespread bunyip myth lies in the fact that from time to time seals have made their way up the winding waters of the Murray and Darling rivers and the vast network of associated streams, to live there for a time in the billabongs and lagoons. More than ninety years ago a seal was actually shot in a lagoon near Conargo, New South Wales; it was stuffed and remained over the chimney-place at the Conargo Hotel for many years. This animal had penetrated over nine hundred miles inland along the streams of the Murray basin.

The mysterious booming sound made by the bittern, a very shy bird, has become associated with the bunyip, but actual observers have usually described the sound of the latter as a roar or bellow.

The imagination of the Port Phillip Aborigines pictured the bunyip as a fearsome booming beast, as big as a bullock, with an emu's neck, the mane and tail of a horse, and a seal's flippers. It had a cuckoo's instinct, and laid turtle's eggs in the nest of a platypus. Strangely enough the description fits very closely that extinct marine reptile the plesiosaurus. But the bunyip, unlike the plesiosaurus, when it tired of crayfish, ate blacks!

In any case it seems that the fabled bunyip has at least some slight substratum of fact.

The following news item appeared in the Melbourne *Morning Herald* of 29th October 1849:

'The Veritable Bunyip has been seen at last! We are informed by Mr Edwards, the managing clerk at the office of Messrs Moor and Chambers, that during his late trip, and making the circuit of Phillip Island, he and his party were astonished at observing an animal sitting upon a bank in a lake.

'The animal is described as being from 6–7 feet long [about 2 metres] and, in general appearance, half man and half baboon.

'Five shots were fired, and the last discharge was replied to by a spring into the air, and a contemptuous fling out of the hind legs, and a final disappearance in the placid waters of the lake. A somewhat long neck, feathered like an emu, was the peculiar characteristic of the animal.'

The natives believed that the bunyip would engulf solitary fishermen, canoe and all, in its vast jaws and then sink like a stone to its undiscoverable den. An early Australian writer mentioned that six Aborigines preferred death by bushfire to taking shelter in a waterhole said to be the home of a bunyip.

POLLY McQUINN'S WATERHOLE

One of the oldest spooks in Australia concerns Polly McQuinn's Waterhole in the Victorian district of Strathbogie, not far from Euroa. Many and varied are the stories about Polly and the waterhole. Polly McQuinn was a niece of Pollock McQuinn, a pioneer of the district. One day she set out for Euroa to purchase household necessities. While in Euroa the stream rose. When she was returning the current was so strong that it swept her into the waterhole and she was never again seen. Ever since the waterhole has been called Polly McQuinn's Waterhole. On a moonlight night, every seven years, so the legend goes, Polly makes her appearance.

TASMANIAN GHOSTS

Tasmania probably has more ghosts to the square mile than any other State. This may be due to its early settlement and the violence practised under the brutal convict system. In 1834 on a well-known property at Campbell Town a butler dropped a silver tray containing china. For this misdemeanour he was flogged to death. Each year on the anniversary of his demise, it is said, you can hear the crash of the dropped tray. In the same district a madman was bricked up in a little cottage for his own and the community's safety, and for many years after his death his frenzied screams were heard at night. In the neighbouring township of Ross is a summer house in which a coffin lit by burning candles appears. This manifestation is said to perpetuate an accidental death by drowning.

In these districts and others such as Latrobe, Fingal and Richmond nobody sets out deliberately to prove the presence of ghosts. They are accepted and tolerated. Generally the stories of their origin are there for the asking and most likely they are supported by history. It is claimed that there are two haunted bridges in Tasmania—the Richmond Bridge, which incidentally is the oldest in Australia, and a bridge in the Fingal district.

More than a century ago Richmond was a stop-over place for coaches running from Hobart to the east coast. There were nine inns in those days, but only two remain now. In the pleasant valley stand mellow homes and buildings including St John's Church, which is claimed to be the oldest Roman Catholic church in Australia. The placid river makes a charming setting for the Richmond Bridge ghost. Many stories are told of this apparition which people claim to have seen both in daylight and dark, sometimes appearing as a man with a strange headdress and sometimes as a man with no head on him at all.

According to the Tasmanian historian, Karl von Stieglitz, OBE, there was a violent death on the bridge during the course of its construction. The convicts who built it were in the charge of an overseer tyrannical in the matter of punishment. He naturally aroused among the convicts bitter hatred and desire for revenge. So when the bridge was finished they murdered him and threw his body into the river below.

The second haunted bridge spans the Break of Day river at Cullenswood, Fingal. One story tells of the occasion when several farmers were awaiting the arrival of a shearing gang from the mainland, and were watching the bridge over which the gang would come. There was nobody on the bridge when the shearers' car approached it. The farmers saw it slow down and heard its horn blast and were mystified at the reason. When the shearers disembarked they asked the farmers, 'What happened to the woman we saw on the bridge with the pram? Where did she go?'

The answer to that, old inhabitants say, is found in the records of the early days when a convict nurse pushing a pram containing a baby boy fell off the bridge into the river, both being drowned. This happened in 1830; the baby belonged to a prominent family of farmers.

In the district of Avoca stands Garth, an old home with a spine-chilling reputation. The home has never been lived in, nor was it ever finished by the workmen. In keeping with its tradition of ghosts, it gives an impression both forlorn and sinister.

The sombre two-storeyed stone building stands on the bank of the South Esk, not far from Fingal. Early in the last century a young settler engaged to a girl in England built the house for his prospective bride. So anxious was he to bring her to his 'dream-home' that he sailed for England before the house was completed. On arrival in England he found she had married someone else. He returned to Avoca, and, in a fit of dejection, committed suicide in the courtyard of the unfinished building.

Behind the courtyard are the remains of a well which also added its story to the tragedy of Garth. It is said that a child rushed towards the well in fear when her nurse, a convict woman, threatened her with dire punishment for misbehaviour. In her terror the child jumped in and was drowned, and the nurse, attempting to rescue her, was drowned also. The graves are in the grounds nearby. The upstairs rooms and hall of Garth are still unfinished as the builders left them.

In his book on Latrobe, Mr von Stieglitz tells a few stories about this ghost-ridden district.

'From the "Old Stone House",' he writes, 'which stands on a property not far from the sea, strange occurrences have been recorded over the years. In this stone house an old man, reputedly a miser, was strangled to death for gold many years ago, but the murderer was never caught. While the "Old Stone House", which stands on the edge of a forest, was at the height of its ghost fame, a young man with a dog drove up one night in a car. He left the car standing in the road with the dog on guard, and managed with difficulty to open a back door and enter. He mounted the stairs to the second storey, striking matches so that he could see where the old flooring boards were missing or broken. He was determined to investigate the evil reports of the old place, but had made no particular arrangements for the visit to the building, which had stood empty since abandoned by its last fear-ridden tenants.

'When he reached the top of the stairs he entered the right hand room at the front of the house and seated himself in a comer with his back to a wall. He stayed there patiently listening and watching for some time without anything unusual happening. He was about to give up, being satisfied that there was nothing which could not be accounted for other than the rustling of old papers on the floor or the creaking of rotting timbers, when he heard a pattering of feet on the stairs, and a moment later felt a cold, wet nose in his hand. The little dog had come to search for him.

'He stroked the dog and was about to descend the stairs when the dog broke into a frenzy of barking. Then it hurled itself into a corner of the room near the door opening on to the staircase, and the young man anxiously fumbled for his matches. While he was getting a match he could hear sounds of a violent struggle, and then the dog's barks changed to choking, sobbing efforts to breathe, which suddenly ceased. When the young man managed to strike a match all he could see was the dead body of the dog huddled in the corner.

'On a property not far from the sea which had best be nameless, for strange things may still be seen and heard there by those known as "sensitives", the Grey Lady used to appear. She wore grey, old-fashioned clothes, had grey hair and skin. She used to move in dark corridors as twilight fell, smiling sadly, or pass through rooms at night on soundless feet, never happy and never at rest. When several visitors had been deeply affected by the sight of her, it was decided to get a church dignitary to exorcise her, so that she could find peace. After the service, which is an old form of church service for use in such cases, and which includes prayers for peace for the afflicted soul, nobody saw the old Grey Lady again.'

DEVLIN'S GHOST

In the early days of settlement in South Australia cattle-duffers and convicts often used to escape from New South Wales to South Australia by crossing the Murray River at Overland Corner and heading for the Mount Lofty Ranges. One of these cattle-duffers was an Irishman named Devlin. He started a wine shanty not far from Overland Corner. It was a secluded spot, with green river-flats hemmed in by great cliffs, where cattle-duffers brought stolen herds and skinned them for their hides.

Whenever a drover made merry at his shanty Devlin's men stole some of the grazing cattle and took them to a secret hiding-place. Next morning the unfortunate drover always started off short of a hundred or so cattle. Devlin amassed a fortune this way. Overland

Corner soon became famous as a paradise for 'Poddy Dodgers'.

Devlin disappeared one night and was never seen again. Fifty years later an Adelaide professor, digging for specimens in an Aboriginal graveyard near Overland Corner, found a long white box four feet under the ground. Opening it he found the body of a tall white man with a red beard and red hair. And near the right ear was a bullet hole. It was Devlin. Someone had had his revenge on the tough old Irishman. But his ghost returned to haunt the drovers, and even today around the camp fires they tell the story of a ghost rider on a white horse who appears suddenly at night to stampede cattle. And when cattle stray in the area today they still say: 'Devlin's ghost took them!'

Murdering Sandhills

A disturbing sound is that of the ghostly wagonette which is sometimes trundled across the ridge known as Murdering Sand hills near Narrandera, New South Wales. Drovers have often reported hearing the frightening rumble at night. Those who have not known its eerie origin have been so sure that it was an approaching wagon that they have made a lane through their camped sheep to let it pass. It is said to echo the sounds of a tragic night in the 1870s when three men murdered two brothers named Pollman. The Pollman brothers were hawkers who were thought to have a large sum of money hidden in their wagonette. The murderers did not find the money they were seeking but they turned the horses loose and trundled the wagonette into the creek. Apparently in the next world they have been condemned to a continual repetition of the profitless performance.

Ghosts of Cooper's Creek

The most noteworthy haunt of ghosts in the outback country, according to the distinguished Australian writer Ernestine Hill, is in that part of western Queensland where many rivers flow down to Cooper's Creek. 'You can read a book by the light of the ghosts anywhere on the Cooper in the evening,' a Windorah stockman told Mrs Hill. 'Pretty well every station has a ghost or two about.'

The pioneers of the Cooper country were Celtic folk, fey and vividly imaginative. Their descendants have inherited an emotional faith in

the supernatural, and a quick eye for a chimera or ghost. Apparently they are surrounded by a lively diversity of creatures in psychic phenomena that are often seen and heard and quite interesting to meet.

Along the river banks are many railed-in graves recalling tragic deaths by flood and drought. Nine men are buried at Innamincka Crossing, the home of the ghost of Robert O'Hara Burke, the explorer, who died of starvation at Quibidee Waterhole. In this lonely setting the grieving wandering spirit of Burke may be seen most times alongside the tree marked with his initials near where he died.

Dead Man Crossing, near Windorah, was the scene of five drowning fatalities. A railed-in grave on a sandhill near the station is the burial place of a youth named Euston whose mother saw him swept to his death. Sometimes the grave is submerged by floodwaters and at other times engulfed by big dust-storms, but it is always there again, the landmark of the four posts. Many have seen a glowing light that rambles the sandhill as though always searching for something. On the same station property, where Ned Hammond was thrown from his mettlesome horse and killed, his ghost still rides on. Travellers by motor-car have seen him in the glare of the headlights as he goes riding by in a whirlwind, and if they camp they hear him galloping—forever galloping through the night.

At Kyabra, near Thylungra, a woman walks the creek in the moonlight. According to local reports, the tall and imperious spectre is that of Mrs Webber, who once ruled the station with a rod of iron. She was buried there on her favourite little plot of lawn facing the front door. Later occupants of the home disapproved of the grave in such a conspicuous place and had it removed elsewhere. From that day to this the self-willed ghost of Mrs Webber has never rested.

Gilpippie Ghost is the wraith of a stockman which flits through the coolibah trees on Tanbar station. The stockman shot his mate, some say accidentally, some say in the heat of a quarrel over a girl. He raised the gun and said, 'Where will you have it?' His mate laughed and pointed to his forehead. 'Right here in the curl,' he said. He got it. The stockman was acquitted; it could not be proved that he knew the gun was loaded. But crazed with remorse and melancholy, he jumped into the Gilpippie Waterhole.

Dick Grosvenor haunts the Munro Plain. He was a fine old English gentleman who acted as schoolmaster to the station children. Eighty years old, and weighing over 18 stone (114 kilograms), he was beloved by all. One day, alone at the homestead, he went to get a dish of flour from the 200 lb (90 kilogram) bag, fell into the bag head first, could not regain his footing, and was stifled in flour. 'The old cove with the big white whiskers down to his waist' was often seen by people who knew nothing of him in life and apparently the 18-stone ghost still likes to wander round the station property.

AUSTRALIA'S MOST HAUNTED HOUSE

Historic Bungaribee House, Doonside, 23 miles (37 kilometres) west of Sydney, received its death knell in 1957 when the property of 774 acres (313 hectares) was purchased by a radio transmission station and the 131-year-old homestead handed over to the demolishers.

Distinguished by the graceful beauty of its stately colonial architecture, the white two-storey homestead with its wide columned verandah stood on top of a slight rise surrounded by well-kept lawns and gardens and shaded by hedges of pink oleander shrubs, the blue drooping blooms of wisteria and tall pine trees. It contained a spacious entrance hall and the lofty rooms of polished cedar included a ballroom, reception rooms, servants' quarters, store room, ham house, stables, barns, blacksmiths' shops and 'superior barracks for the men'. All of it was dominated by a 'round convict-watching tower' in front where French windows looked out across the charming grounds.

Bungaribee witnessed many a romantic scene, with twirling crinolines, fluttering fans, the glint of swords and scarlet uniforms in the ballroom and couples strolling on the cool lawns. But Bungaribee had also more than its share of tragedy. Indeed, it always had a sinister association.

Built by Major John Campbell in 1826, with convict labour, it is said that the bricks were brought specially from England and that they were drawn in hand-carts by women convicts from Sydney harnessed in pairs. Neither Campbell nor his wife ever lived in Bungaribee, for both died before it was completed. The site of the home is ground which was sacred to the Aborigines. The very name Bungaribee is a native one meaning 'the burial ground of a great chief'. Its tragedies include the murder of a convict on the property, the suicide of an officer shot through the heart in one of the upper bedrooms the floor of which bore the bloodstains for generations afterwards, and the mystery death of a colonel found dead in the grounds.

Bungaribee's hauntings and queer happenings were many and varied. One of the earliest tales concerns a youth of seventeen, sturdy and level-headed, who stayed there alone while his family, the owners, were away. He spent the first night in the bedroom which had been unoccupied since the suicide there. He woke up during the night to feel cold hands gripping his throat. He struggled for his life, broke free, and rushed out of the house. He was found next day still shaking with fear in a paddock.

In a letter to the *Sydney Morning Herald* in January 1957, apropos of the proposed demolition of Bungaribee House, Sydney McKeon of Bundeena disclosed the following information on the haunted reputation of the homestead:

'Some fifty years ago, I was employed by Mr Robert Boulden, of Minna Rosa dairy, Enfield, who at the same time held the lease of Bungaribee House and lands, and was using the land as agistment for dry cows from his dairy. This family, which consisted of father, mother, and two sons, had previously resided at Bungaribee, but, because of ghostly manifestations in the house, they decided to move.

'Mrs Boulden (a strict Christian) told me that night after night the family had seen an old man—or so he appeared to be, judging by his bent body—in convict garb and wearing leg-irons, slowly ascending the stairs leading to the tower room, where he would vanish. Again, when members of the family were returning home late at night, this same old lag would be sitting upon one of the gateposts. The horses refused to go through the gateway, and the family had to drive to another entrance.

'On other occasions, on arriving home late, the family saw the tower room (it always remained unoccupied) illuminated by a strange glow.'

Shortly after the publication of this letter, Mrs A. F. Wyatt, of St Ives, vice-president of the National Trust, who lived near Bungaribee for many years, said she remembered seeing the blood-stained bedroom floor. She told journalist David Burke that she had had her own strange experiences in Bungaribee encounters which she prefers to forget. Mrs Wyatt told of a woman who, like the youth, felt the cold clutching hands on her throat. She came to, shivering in a corner, wrapped in a table cloth.

Another story told about the eerie house concerned a child of five who was said to be not at all nervous of the dark. In the middle of the night his parents heard him give a terrible shriek. They found the child crouching on his pillow. His eyes were glassy and he was staring into a corner. 'Don't let him touch me,' he screamed. 'Don't let him come near me!'

Little wonder that Bungaribee House earned the reputation of 'Australia's most haunted house'.

Though most Australian ghosts seem to prefer the open country, the cities have not been without occasional spectres. Famous explorer Sir Thomas Mitchell died in 1855 and was buried from his fine old mansion in Sydney's Darling Point. For years thereafter, some reported hearing a ghostly carriage clatter to the door of Sir Thomas's house as it did when he was alive. They heard grunts and movement as if someone were alighting, and also the sound of a door being slammed. They saw nothing, but were ready to swear that it was the ghost of Sir Thomas arriving in its own spirit-world carriage to have a look round the old home.

Melbourne's best known ghost is probably that of Federici, prominent Italian basso. Federici collapsed and died when appearing as Mephistopheles in *Faust* at the Princess Theatre one night in 1888. Beautiful, well-loved Nellie Stewart and other players rushed to his side when he fell. Federici was beyond aid.

A few days later he was buried. Then began his ghostly returns, according to scores of people, to Spring Street and the Princess Theatre. He was sometimes seen on stage and in the wings. Generally he favoured an empty seat in the dress circle, where he could watch the performance. Still clad in his flowing cape and dress of Mephistopheles, he was frequently mistaken for an actor in the company appearing on stage. Gradually his visits became less frequent. It is some years now since Federici's ghost last appeared.

Lady Binney, wife of the retiring Governor of Tasmania, returned to England in 1951. Her most enduring memory of Australia was the ghost she heard about the corridors of the century-old Government House in Hobart during her five-year stay. On many occasions, she revealed, eerie moaning voices echoed through the ancient residence. Often they were followed by a ghostly voice which always gave the same message, 'It's a quarter past eleven.' Exhaustive investigation never solved the mystery of the time-conscious wraith. Her ladyship returned to her homeland convinced that Australia was better served with ghosts than most people imagined.

A well-known residence reputed to be haunted is the palace of the

Anglican Bishop at Broome, Western Australia. A Bishop and others have made public statements that they saw a ghostly figure in the spacious old-fashioned bungalow used as the Bishop's Palace. The ghost is presumed to be a formerly well-known Jewish pearl-buyer named Davis, who went down with the steamer *Koombana* between Broome and Fremantle in 1912.

First to see the ghost was the late Bishop Gerard Trower, who woke one night to see a wraithlike figure in a patch of light. The figure was in the robe and headgear of a Jewish rabbi. When the Bishop called, it vanished. Davis acted as rabbi for the small Jewish community of Broome. He had owned the bungalow, later transformed into the Bishop's Palace. Some assumed he returned to keep an eye on a hoard of pearls he was said to have hidden on the premises.

The Guyra Ghost

One of the most inexplicable and most recent of well testified Australian ghosts is the invisible poltergeist in the New South Wales town of Guyra in 1921. For about a month the household of a local council worker suffered almost nightly disturbances that seemed to have a ghostly origin. Stones were thrown through windows. The walls of the cottage rocked as if under sledge-hammer blows. Police and volunteers by the score kept nightly watch. The attacks continued, seemingly without human agency.

For a while suspicion fell on the 12-year-old daughter of the house. It was soon obvious, however, that she was guiltless, for the attacks continued while she was under observation. After a month, quiet again descended on the house. Psychic researchers were convinced a poltergeist was responsible. No other satisfactory explanation could be offered by the police or anyone else—either for the attacks on the house or the mysterious vanishing at the time of an 87-year-old Irishwoman, Mrs Doran, who was never seen again.

Of all Australia's ghosts, none caused greater argument and discussion than the affair at Guyra.

TREASURE TROVE

From Spanish Shores; Dog God Idol; Ship with a Silver Keel;
One Chance in a Million; Stolen Gold; Warrior Island;
Batavia Mutiny; Dutch Ship Zuytdorp; Benito Benita's Treasure;
Tullaree Treasure; Nicholson Fortune; Sedlitz Treasure; Tennant's Gold;
Snowy River Gold; Cloncurry Gold; Coorong Treasure;
Lord Howe Island's Buried Treasure; Legend of the Silver Reef.

The Islands of North Australia, especially in the Torres Strait, are a fascinating field for treasure trove. Some of the old Spanish shipwrecks have been seen by the pearl divers and a fair amount of their treasures recovered. Most of it, however, now lies smothered beneath coral.

Some years ago Frank Jardine, a well-known pearler, found beneath the rusty anchor of one of these wrecks a small fortune in ancient Spanish gold coins. On Stephens Island a fisherman found a native idol which was decorated with valuable old Castilian jewellery. Then again, on Prince of Wales Island a crumbling skeleton was found, alongside of which was a huge rusty sword of ancient Spanish design. Near by was a valuable gold goblet.

Quite a number of gold coins have been found on Booby Island. In the early days Booby Island was the headquarters of the only real pirates that Australia has ever known. They were a band of Asiatic cut-throats who plundered the Spanish treasure ships as they sailed to and from the Philippines. The buccaneers were finally wiped out in a sea battle with a Spanish man-o'-war, but their valuable loot is thought to be buried somewhere on Booby. That lonely island is riddled with caves, some of which have never been explored. Maybe the pirates' hoard is hidden in one of them.

Last century Booby Island was a regular calling-place for all the sailing vessels plying to and from Australia via Torres Strait. There is very little to be seen today on the island to remind one of its importance, save one curiosity—a cave that was used as a post-office. It was an arrangement between the captains and crews whereby they used to drop their letters into a box that was kept in the cave. When a ship called the captain would open the box and, if there were any letters for his run, collect them. Alongside the seamen's letterbox was a big diary. In this the captains signed and entered the dates their ships called. The letter-box is still there but the diary has vanished. The only records to be seen are hundreds of names of seamen and their ships scratched on the walls of the cave. At one time the Queensland Government always kept in this unattended post-office food, water and clothing for shipwrecked sailors.

Dog God Idol

Not all the hidden treasures of Torres Strait are from the old Spanish wrecks. Secreted somewhere on Moa Island is an ancient and valuable tortoise-shell idol that was once worshipped by the former savage warriors there. The idol was the famous Dog God of Moa. It was a huge and remarkable figure of a dog. About 20 feet long and 12 feet high (6 x 3.5 metres); modelled in thick tortoise-shell; more than two hundred of the finest tortoise-shells were used in its construction.

The missionaries began their work in the Torres Strait during the early 1880s. When rumours reached the natives of Moa about these strange white men who destroyed the old gods and idols, the chiefs determined to safeguard the Dog God. They carried the great idol to a secret cave and sealed up the entrance to it. Then they made a pledge never to reveal its whereabouts to any white man. Those who knew of its hiding-place are now dead, and they have taken the secret with them to the grave.

It is now believed that a landslide in past years must have covered the entrance to the Dog God's home, hiding the idol forever from the prying eyes of man.

Ship with a Silver Keel

The natives of Murray Island tell a tale of a ship with a silver keel which was wrecked off the island a long time ago. They say that every person aboard the ship was massacred by the fierce natives of those days. The legend is emphatic that the keel of the vessel was of solid silver—a rich prize to the finder. Unfortunately the natives have a deep, superstitious dread of the wreck and refuse to guide treasure seekers to its whereabouts. Some years ago a white official found a group of native children on Murray Island using large Spanish gold pieces as counters in a game in which flat beans usually serve as this medium.

Among the natives, apart from the stories they tell of white men who came in ships, there is definite evidence that large groups of white men have spent much time among them. Some of the island tribes have a strangely light skin with pronounced Latin features. Moreover, Spanish words are included in their dialects.

One Chance in a Million

One of the strangest tales of the Torres Strait—and literally true—

concerns the schooner *Lancashire Lass* that struck a reef on one of the Barrier Reef islands in 1890.

The vessel laden with pearl-shell was returning to a Queensland port from the pearling grounds east of Cape York. A gale blew up, but the schooner flew before it and made fast time on the homeward course, for she was a good sea boat and skilfully handled. And then, with startling suddenness, there loomed, immediately ahead, great surges piling up and breaking in walls of foam—a sure indication of the weather side of a coral-reef.

It was a terrifying sight, and to change course was quite impossible.

All the skipper could do was to look for a gap in the reef through which he might attempt a passage. But there was no gap; look as he might, he could see nothing but a wall of surf stretching right across the course from one extreme to the other of the limited horizon. There was nothing to be done except to keep the plunging schooner at it, in the desperate hope that some great wave might lift the vessel over the wall.

The one chance in a million came off; as the little craft approached the reef and almost inevitable destruction, a huge comber roared up behind her and carried her over the obstruction into the calmness of the lagoon on the other side. The sails were lowered, and the anchor let go. The schooner rode in safety, while all hands thanked their lucky stars for such unexpected good fortune.

Next day, wind and sea were fairly normal. It now became necessary to find a way out, but, after exploring all round the coral barrier, no gap could be discovered through which the schooner might pass to the open sea. The only hope of escape lay in putting the cargo of pearl-shell overboard, so that the ship might be sufficiently lightened to be floated across the reef at high tide.

This was done; the shell was sewn up in bags and lowered over the side to the bottom of the lagoon, into a depth of about 30 feet of water. The site of the cargo was marked by a buoy, and the geographical position determined. At the next high tide, the schooner managed to scrape over the reef and made the Queensland coast in a few days.

When, on arriving at her home port, the story was told, the owners fitted out another and lighter vessel, and with an experienced diver on board this ship sailed for the spot where the cargo had been jettisoned. The reef was crossed safely, and the buoy found. The anchor dropped, the diver was sent below to begin his job.

A few minutes passed without any signal from him, and then he came up again, making signs for his helmet to be unscrewed.

His story created a sensation; the bags of shell were there right enough, but, he said, they were lying on top of a great mound piled up above the floor of the lagoon, and this mound was composed entirely, as far as he could make out, of silver coins.

To convince the sceptics, he took from the pocket of his diver's dress a lump of Spanish dollars all cemented together by the coral insects, but quite easily separated into individual coins.

There was no delay in beginning the task of raising the loot. There were thousands of dollars there; the schooner had to make several voyages before all the treasure was salvaged.

Consider the miraculous chance that led to the discovery! How the coin got into the lagoon no one can answer with any certainty. Probably a Spanish ship on her way to the Philippines was wrecked on the outer reef and at some time lifted bodily over the coral wall into the shallow water inside. Then, in the course of long years, the ship disintegrated, until nothing was left but the most valuable and imperishable part of her lading—the treasure of silver dollars.

Stolen Gold

Somewhere about Mosman heights in suburban Sydney is buried a fortune that will make the finder affluent for life. The amount is said to be more than £20,000.

The money is the proceeds of Australia's first bank robbery when, on 15th September 1826, the Sydney branch of the Bank of Australia was robbed. The money was never recovered, but it was expertly planted in the vicinity of Mosman heights, so it was said.

Midway between Melbourne and Ballarat still lies hidden the secret hoard of Captain Melville. That bushranger reaped a wealth of treasure from the proceeds of his daring robberies, all of which he concealed in a remote hiding-place. When he was captured he openly boasted that his booty was so well planted that it would defy discovery for hundreds of years.

It is doubtless hidden somewhere in the country where Melville operated, and should be a considerable fortune. Included amongst the treasure hunters who have sought in vain to find it was Marcus Clarke, author of the Australian classic, *For the Term of His Natural Life*. He put arduous toil into searching some of the caves in the Grampian Mountains.

Other bushrangers known to have buried the proceeds of their robberies are Ben Hall, Thunderbolt, and Frank Gardiner. Ben Hall's booty is believed to be hidden in the depths of the beautiful Bungonia Caves, about twenty-five miles out of Goulburn. Thunderbolt's spoil is said to be somewhere in the Mudgee ranges.

A strange sequel is told about the loot of Frank Gardiner 'King of the Bushrangers'. Gardiner is the only bushranger buried outside Australia. When he was freed from prison he decided to go to America. There, in the United States, he became quite a respected citizen.

He had operated as a bushranger in the Forbes district. A few years after his death in America there came to Forbes three husky young Americans. They did not give their names, or mention anything about themselves other than the fact that they were brothers. Soon after their arrival in the district they discovered in the hilly country a hoard of bushrangers' gold. The men then packed up and returned to America.

After their departure some old residents of Forbes recalled the strong resemblance of the young men to Frank Gardiner, and now it is believed that they were his sons. Perhaps he told them where he had hidden the gold and, after his death, they decided to retrieve it.

Presumably the loot was not that of the Eugowra robbery, when Gardiner and his gang bailed up the gold escort and robbed it of £10,000. What became of that plunder is a mystery, but, according to a story, there is good reason for believing that two enterprising Scotsmen 'sprung' the bushrangers' loot, and got away with it to their native land. In recent years an account was published concerning a man named Percy Faithful who, when in Scotland in 1904, was shown a cottage and told a strange tale about the man living in it.

This Scot, and a friend of his, had emigrated to Australia in their young days. One night, when tramping through the country looking for work, they sought shelter in a hut, whose sole occupant was a woman. The request for a night's lodging was refused, the woman saying that the bushrangers were likely to return at any moment, and they might suspect the travellers of being police spies.

Even as she spoke the gang appeared in the distance and the woman hurriedly locked the two travellers in a small room. The bushrangers, who were in a desperate hurry (police being on their tracks) handed to the woman a bag full of gold, told her to 'plant' it, and then rode away. The Scotsmen, so the story goes, took the gold from the defenceless woman and cleared out. With their doubly ill-gotten booty, to the value of £10,000, the precious pair boarded at Sydney a vessel bound for the Old Country, which they reached safely, to enjoy the golden fruits of the Eugowra escort robbery. That is the tale.

WARRIOR ISLAND

Much has been written about the great pearling industry of Australia's northern tropical seas, but little has been said of the romantic Torres Strait island that was the birthplace of the industry. Forgotten, too, is the name of Captain Banner, who, in 1868, discovered the first pearls, but whose untimely death prevented him from sharing in the fortunes that were amassed by the majority of the pioneer pearlers. Today the name of that island is Warrior Island.

In the early days, Warrior Island was known by its native name of

Tute. It was the home of hostile natives—noted sea warriors whose powerful fleet of huge outrigger canoes was feared throughout Torres Strait and along the coast of New Guinea. All native trading vessels travelling between New Guinea and the mainland had to pay the Warrior Islanders a 'toll' in goods before they were allowed to pass; any vessel that refused to pay was promptly sunk and the natives on board killed.

Strangely enough, the first white men to visit the island received an enthusiastic reception; they were the crew of a French ship, which, in distress, called there in 1790 to repair a damaged rudder. The natives gave the visitors every assistance and treated the sailors like kings. Unfortunately the Frenchmen sailed away without offering the natives anything whatsoever for their services. This unfair treatment incensed the islanders so much that from then on they attacked every white man's boat that neared their territory.

It was not warfare that finally subdued the sea warriors. In the early sixties of last century Captain Moresby of the HMS *Basilisk* managed to make friends with them by giving them presents of tobacco and other trade goods when he encountered them at sea. Later, in 1868, Captain Banner happened to call at the island and was amazed to see all the natives—men, women and children—wearing strings and ornaments of valuable pearls. The children were even using pearls for marbles.

When Captain Banner's story reached civilisation, the great pearl rush commenced to the then lonely and little-known seas of Australia's northern coasts. Gradually the pearl-beds of Warrior Island were worked out, and since the year 1900 the island has been forgotten.

In pearl fishing, hardship and endeavour, joys and disappointments, humour and tragedy, go hand in hand. There was one northern pearler who discovered a perfect, round pearl which was valued at £10,000. He gave the gem to his wife to guard for him until the end of the pearling season, when he intended making a special journey to London to sell it. His wife placed the pearl for safe keeping in a small bottle, which she hung on a chain around her neck, inside her dress. Then Fate intervened. On the pearler's last trip to sea for the season, his wife accompanied him, but the boat foundered during a cyclone, and all on board were drowned, with the exception of the pearler himself. His wife, with the bottle containing the pearl still hanging around her neck, went down with the boat, and although divers spent many weeks searching for her body, it was never found. The sea still holds that valuable pearl in its keeping.

Batavia Mutiny

A grim yet fascinating background of murder, mutiny, piracy and treasure, hangs like a sombre mantle over the Abrolhos, a group of rocky islands two hundred miles north of Perth and only a few miles off the Western Australian coast. Houtman's Abrolhos is the full name of the group, their discoverer having been that Frederick Houtman who in the early seventeenth century was engaged by the Dutch East India Company to command a fleet of eleven ships sent from Holland to the far distant Spice Islands, there to negotiate and load for the home market those exotic products which made the East Indies trade so profitable.

The route of the voyage from Amsterdam to Batavia was via the Cape of Good Hope, the east coast of Africa, and across the Indian Ocean—a journey that usually took twelve months. When Houtman and his fleet of vessels set out on the expedition in 1617 he travelled further eastward than he intended and made a landfall on the Western Australian coast where the town of Geraldton now stands. In his journals he describes the land as 'a level, broken country with reefs all around it'. He marked the position of certain islands on his map, and named them the Abrolhos, a Portugese word meaning 'Look out!' The name was prophetic.

Eleven years later, Francis Pelsart was given command of the ship *Batavia* by a group of Amsterdam merchants. The *Batavia* was commissioned to engage in the South Seas trade. She carried a fortune in silver and a wealth of valuable merchandise for trading purposes. She also carried a very mixed company. It included adventurous spirits, both men and women, who were going to Batavia and elsewhere to make their fortunes, and who were not over particular as to the methods they might adopt to gain their ends. The crew was drawn from the scum of the Amsterdam waterfront, and even the officers were not the strongest team that could have been selected.

Trouble was inevitable; it broke out early in the voyage when it became plain that the captain—next in rank to Pelsart—was neglecting his navigation for the women on board. Half the crew put their heads together and planned to take the ship by surprise, throw overboard those who wouldn't join them, and turn pirates. But before this dashing exploit could be carried out, the coast of Western Australia was sighted, and shortly afterwards the ship ran aground on one of the islands of the Abrolhos.

Passengers and crew now found themselves in a hopeless situation on the reefs. They salvaged provisions and chests of money and jewels. It is known that four chests of scarlet, cloth of gold and silver fabrics, and three boxes of silver and antiques were salvaged and stored somewhere on the reefs. A few hundred gallons of water was saved but this would not last long with more than two hundred people. There was no water on any of the islands, and unless it rained it was plain that they would perish. The commander, Pelsart, with the captain and a few officers made a search for water on the mainland of the Western Australian coast but could find none. Pelsart then decided to make the dangerous voyage to Batavia in a small boat to seek help.

When weeks passed and Pelsart failed to return, one of the ship's officers—Cornelius—assumed command with the idea of building a smaller vessel from the timbers of the wreck, and, with a few kindred souls sailing away on a career of piracy. The rest of the castaways, it was decided, would be killed. About fifty cut-throats were selected as

Cornelius's comrades in crime, and an attractive woman was earmarked for each. This important business completed, it was decided that the rest of the ship's company and passengers must be disposed of. The following night about one hundred men and women were massacred. Stabbed or beaten to death, their bodies were thrown into the sea. In celebration of their victory the murderers opened kegs of wine and decked themselves out in rich embroidered velvets and costly silks that had been brought out on the ill-fated vessel for the merchants of Batavia.

But even the most perfectly conceived plans sometimes come unstuck; during the slaughter, a few of the attacked party escaped to one of the adjacent islands. When the would-be pirates got over their drunken orgy they attempted to land on the island where the little band had taken refuge, but the fugitives beat them back each time.

In the meantime Pelsart had reached Batavia, obtained help, and returned to the scene of the shipwreck on board the frigate *Sardam*. A bloody hand-to-hand fight ensued in which all the mutineers were captured. Pelsart had the ringleaders hanged on the spot, after erecting the gallows with his own hands. The rest were taken to Batavia to be dealt with in more conventional fashion.

Before leaving, a start was made to transfer to the *Sardam* the silver aboard the *Batavia*. (The latter vessel did not sink; she remained perched on the treacherous ridge which had broken her back.) A sudden storm sprang up and the *Batavia* broke in two and sank below the waves. To this day, no one has succeeded in raising the treasure.

Dutch Ship *Zuytdorp*

Dozens of pieces of eight were found early in 1955 by a treasure hunting expedition on the rugged north coast of Western Australia. The expedition—a geologist, a skin diver, a bushman, a journalist, and a press photographer—found the wreck of the Dutch ship *Zuytdorp* which ran ashore near the mouth of the Murchison River in 1712. The vessel was lost en route from the Cape of Good Hope to Batavia.

The three-week search also yielded pieces of the ship's mast and other woodwork, musket balls, a 20 lb (9 kg) brass breechblock from cannon, navigation instruments, chests, buckles, buttons, pottery, and a quantity of ducats and stuivers.

Evidence was found which showed that many of the ship's company of about 300 survived the shipwreck and got ashore, but what happened to them remains a mystery. It is possible that the party journeyed north towards Batavia, moved inland in search of water, intermingled with natives, or built another boat from the wreckage of their own ship; or shifting sand on the coastal strip at the cliff-top could have buried their remains.

The wreckage was seen in 1927 by a bushman named Tom Pepper. Pepper, an overseer of Tamala sheep station, one of the few properties in the rugged area, set out to track a dingo which had been raiding the station's flocks. The chase led him 45 miles (72 kilometres) to the coast, a part which, as far as he knew, had never before been visited by a white man.

After Pepper had shot the dingo he rode about a mile along the coast. Like other parts of this seaboard it was almost unbelievably wild. Pepper decided to find a path down the cliff. As he scrambled down he noticed an unusual amount of driftwood, and at the bottom of the cliff he found evidence of a shipwreck—a very old shipwreck.

In the years that followed, Pepper returned to the spot several times and collected about 200 old, silver coins and many items from the wreck, including a ship's figurehead. Weighing about 120 lb (55 kilograms), and beautifully carved in oak, the figurehead is 4 feet 3 inches tall and 1 foot 3 inches thick (130 x 38 centimetres) thick at its widest point. It represents a woman with her face turned upward and backward so that she would be looking across the sea. A wreath is carved behind her head, and immediately under her chin is a carving of a lion with its jaw part-open; it appears to be part of her body.

The treasures lay in Pepper's home unnoticed and neglected until a young geologist, Phillip Playford of the staff of a petroleum company, visited the station. His interest was such that he organised an expedition to search the site of the wreck. The party travelled from Northampton, 342 miles (550 kilometres) north of Perth, to the scene, by utility and jeep.

The men worked along jagged reefs at the foot of towering limestone cliffs up to 800 feet (245 metres) high. The skin diver blasted away part of the reef and some boulders. A handful of coins was found in a 'pocket' and a few loose coins were found in the rubble. Sometimes the men entered caverns beneath the reef. Here also they found coins and parts of a ship's equipment. In all they found 62 coins, which brought the total find from all searches to 400.

'The coins,' said Playford, 'were scattered over about 30 yards (27 metres) of reef and rock. It seems obvious that at one time many thousands of coins were swept about by the waves, both on the reef and in the honeycombing of tunnels under the reef. Without doubt the coins which lodged and stopped there, despite the swirling wash of the waves, formed only a very small percentage of the original number. We think that probably many thousands of coins were swept about the reef at one time, and that most of them were carried out over the edge of the reef by the strong backwash.

'The Dutch sailors were probably unable to take off the treasure chests, which usually were carried deep in the ships of that time. Constant pounding over the years would have broken up the chests. Then the waves may have picked up thousands of coins and showered them over the reef—waves of coins.'

What happened to the crew of the ship from which the treasure came? Did the sailors journey north towards Batavia, or move inland? Were they speared by hostile natives? Or possibly the natives were friendly and they lived on with their tribes? One thing is certain: If they stayed near the wreck and were not helped by natives, they ultimately died of thirst, for the country is hot and waterless.

The shipwrecked sailors certainly spent some time there. The Playford expedition found evidence of fires they had lit near the sea, of drinking parties, of supplies and other objects that were carried ashore, and of a search inland for water. But there were no graves and no skeletons; no sign of a permanent camp; no signs of fighting or of massacre. It is highly improbable that the crew of the *Zuytdorp* had any chance of refloating the stricken ship. If small boats were carried off, it could be assumed that an attempt was made to sail to Batavia for help. But it would have been extremely difficult—if not impossible—to launch a boat and steer it out through the pounding breakers.

The members of the expedition thought it quite possible that the shipwrecked men began building a larger seagoing boat from the remains of the *Zuytdorp*. This belief was based on the fact that although no carpentry tools were found during their extensive search of the area. they found globules of what had been molten brass, and the Dutchmen may have devised a method of melting down metal and of moulding from it parts for the building of a ship.

If the ship was built, two things may have happened: The Dutchmen, by biding their time and waiting for perfect weather conditions, may have got their boat afloat and out to sea. But, if so, they were never heard of again. The second possibility is that the wrecked men, after completing their vessel, were unsuccessful in their attempts to launch it.

The theory that the Dutchmen—or at least some of them were absorbed into a native tribe cannot be dismissed lightly. Mrs Daisy Bates, in her time the greatest authority on the Australian Aborigine, spent some months in the Murchison area in the early 1900s. She remarked on the strong Dutch characteristics of natives there when she wrote: 'I found these types as far out as the headwaters of the Gascoyne and the Murchison Rivers. There was no mistaking the flat, heavy Dutch face, curly fair hair, and heavy, stocky build.'

In 1943 there was further mention of Dutch characteristics in natives when a resident of Shark Bay (a little north of the wreck-site) pointed out in a newspaper article that some natives in the area had flaxen hair and blue eyes. The writer told of a native named Pieter— 'an extraordinary human specimen and the last of the Ingarra tribe'. Pieter was described thus: with a bright blonde beard, not white but bright golden; sturdy, sinuous limbs, decidedly bandy, a noble girth and a passion for the sea—none of these Aboriginal characteristics.

BENITO BENITA'S TREASURE
A syndicate, backed by wealthy graziers, once searched for another lost treasure at Queenscliff, a township on Port Phillip Bay Victoria. The treasure is believed to be gold and other valuables removed from cathedrals in Peru for safety during the war between Chile and Peru in 1815. South American pirate, Benito Benita, is

supposed to have captured the treasure reputed to be worth millions of pounds from the ship which was carrying it to an unknown destination. Benita is believed to have hidden the loot near where Queenscliff now stands, after being chased by a British man-o'-war. Existence of the treasure has been talked of in Queenscliff for many years.

GOTHENBERG GOLD

There is said to be a fortune in gold to be picked up near Nares Rock, which lies off the coast of North Queensland. The steamer *Gothenberg* was wrecked there on 24th February 1875. On board were more than eighty miners, all of whom had large sums in gold in their possession. There was also £30,000 of gold in the ship's safe. Most of the miners were drowned when the ship sank because they refused to part with their heavy money belts, and thus weighted down they went to the bottom like stones. Their skeletons lie scattered about the wreck today in a hundred fathoms of water, far beyond the reach of divers.

TULLAREE TREASURE

A treasure hoard waiting to be found is reputed to be buried near Tullaree, in Victoria. It is believed to have been put there by a German carpenter named Weiburg, who broke into the strong-room on the ship *Avoca* in the 1870s and got away with 50,000 sovereigns. He escaped from the vessel at Melbourne and made his way to Tullaree where he purchased a farm. Eventually the law caught up with him, but although the police succeeded in recovering more than a thousand of the missing sovereigns, they could not persuade the German to divulge where he had hidden the rest. Local legends assert that they lie buried somewhere on the farm, but although many people have dug for them they have had no success.

NICHOLSON FORTUNE

A fortune is said to be buried somewhere on Savage Hill, near Inverloch, Victoria. An evangelist named Donald Nicholson claimed that many years ago his grandfather had hidden several chests containing gold dust, gems, jade and other valuables in a secret vault somewhere within the hill. It had, it was claimed, all been looted from Chinese temples. For sixteen years Nicholson, known as 'the Inverloch hermit', burrowed into the hill, but when he died in 1954 the treasure vault still defied discovery.

SEDLITZ TREASURE

The sudden outbreak of war with Germany in 1914 was responsible for a German captain burying a quantity of gold and valuables on the north coast of New South Wales. On board the German steamer *Sedlitz* was a large quantity of jewellery, diamonds and gold, worth many thousands of pounds. It was being taken to Germany on behalf of wealthy Germans residing in New South Wales. The captain considered that he would not be able to get to Germany with his valuable cargo, so he pulled in somewhere in the vicinity of Ballina, on the north coast of New South Wales, and buried the treasure. There is no record of it ever being reclaimed after the war.

TENNANT'S GOLD

Within the Australian Capital Territory is a peak named after a bushranger—Mt Tennant. According to local legend, Tennant buried twenty pickle bottles full of sovereigns, as well as a quantity of gold nuggets, at the foot of a dead tree on this mountain. When the bushranger was captured he told the police that he would tell them where he had hidden the gold if they would release him, but Tennant was executed and the gold remains hidden somewhere on Mt Tennant. There are thousands of dead trees in the vicinity, so digging beneath every tree would, indeed, be a big job.

SNOWY RIVER GOLD

Old-timers in the southern Monaro district of New South Wales tell a story of a rusty pick and shovel marking the spot where lies buried the biggest nugget of gold ever seen there. It seems that two prospectors set out from Dalgety to search for gold and returned some time later carrying small gold nuggets and some pieces of gold that they said they had broken off the biggest nugget ever seen in this country. The nugget was far too big for them to carry so they had buried it leaving a pick and a shovel to mark the spot. They were so elated that they 'shouted' for all hands many times—in fact one of the finders died two days later from the effects. When his partner recovered from his celebrations he set out with a party to find the nugget again. Though they searched for months through the rough country the nugget could not be found. He spent the rest of his life searching fruitlessly and finally died of a broken heart.

CLONCURRY GOLD

A mystery Eldorado is said to lie in the Cloncurry district of north-western Queensland. In 1914 a veteran prospector named Mikolite was brought into Cloncurry suffering from fever. It was not until several weeks later when he knew he was going to die that he told a remarkable story about a rich gold reef he had found between Cloncurry and Georgetown, in the mountain ranges near Fiery Down and Lorraine stations. No notice was taken of his story until a few weeks later a civilised Aborigine known as Arthur arrived in Cloncurry claiming that he knew the place where the dead prospector had found gold. Nothing was done about it until after World War I when a local businessman organised a party to search for the reef, but no trace of it was found. Since then others have also tried and failed. However, old-timers who knew the prospector firmly believe that his story was true.

COORONG TREASURE

Somewhere along the lonely Coorong coast of South Australia lies treasure from the ill-fated brigantine *Marie*. The little vessel, with fifteen passengers, the captain and his wife and a crew of nine, left Port Adelaide for Hobart Town on 7th June 1840. The cargo included more than 4,000 English sovereigns. In Lacepede Bay, near Kingston, the *Marie* was holed on the rocks.

Hostile, spear-armed natives awaited the survivors on the beach. The captain held out a handful of gold coins as a peace offering, but the natives showed little interest. He then dangled his silver watch and chain before their eyes and was relieved to see the natives look surprised and appreciative. Quickly some of the passengers and crew produced watches and chains and indicated by sign language that they wanted to reach the nearest white settlement. The leader of the natives nodded his assent and so they all set off in the direction of a whaling station, 120 miles (193 kilometres) away.

Day after day they trudged along the beach, sometimes in blinding rain and sandstorms. Nevertheless, their fears of the wild natives were diminishing. At the head of Lake Albert—three days' journey from the whaling station—they came to the Coorong. Here the leader of the natives indicated that the party must be divided to cross the Coorong in log canoes.

One half made the crossing and, thus divided, the natives clubbed to death all but one of the twenty-six men, women and children. The one who escaped was a woman who reached the Murray mouth, swam the dangerous river and then disappeared forever. However, for years afterwards there were tales of a white woman with red hair living among the Aborigines of the Lower Murray.

The story of the *Marie* massacre reached civilisation through friendly natives. A police-party investigated and found most of the bodies and many personal belongings. The treacherous natives were caught and four of them hanged. What became of the cargo of sovereigns remains a mystery.

LORD HOWE ISLAND'S BURIED TREASURE

Lord Howe Island boasts a tale of treasure trove. Towering far above the rest of the island are two great peaks—Mount Gower at 2,840 feet (865 metres) and Mount Lidgbird at 2,504 feet (763 metres). Around the base of these mountains pandanus and palm forests close in with jungle-like thickness. The story goes that when the whaling brig *George* ran short of water and put in at Lord Howe Island in 1830, she struck a rock in a deep bay and foundered. The vessel carried bullion to the extent of more than 5,000 sovereigns, the result of a previous successful expedition, and before it sank the captain managed to remove the precious cargo ashore. Believing the island to be inhabited by wild natives, although it was in reality uninhabited, the castaways buried their treasure at a particular spot near the south base of Mount Gower.

Eventually they were rescued by another whaling vessel which also put in for water. Not wishing to disclose the whereabouts of the bullion to his rescuers, the captain decided to leave the treasure temporarily behind.

The following year he and his men found an opportunity to return to the island. To their amazement and dismay, they found that during their absence the entire shape of the bay had changed—an immense landslide had avalanched down, completely burying under thousands of tons of basalt rock the site where the bullion had been deposited.

Landslides are by no means uncommon on the precipitous faces of these two mountains; many a one has torn down from the heights since that fateful one. Because the exact spot where the treasure lies buried is unknown, and the hopeless nature of the search is certain, there has never been a treasure-seeking expedition organised to retrieve Lord Howe's lost riches.

Legend of the Silver Reef

In the north-western Australian coastal country, somewhere between King Sound and Wyndham, lies a legendary silver reef; a rich silver lode said to have been discovered by a certain Malay merchant named Hadji Ibrahim some two hundred years ago. From May to October each year Ibrahim fished the then uncharted and unnamed Australian north-west coast for trepang, trochus, tortoise and pearl shell. But while his crew fished, Ibrahim prospected the adjacent country in search of minerals. On one of these expeditions he discovered a reef of silver ore and loaded his prahu with some sixty tons of it which he sold in Macassar for gold to the value of £6,000. The Malayan merchant's luck was shortlived. On his next voyage to these shores he and his vessel vanished with all hands.

Credence is given to the strange story by the fact that Ibrahim kept a journal of all his business transactions and voyages, and these have been carefully preserved by his family to this day. The last journal completed before he sailed into oblivion records the discovery of the silver reef and all particulars about the quantity taken aboard the prahu and its sale to Lie Soe Nyan of Macassar.

Unfortunately the journal gives no indication of the location of the reef, but it is known definitely that he fished the Australian coast between King Sound and the present site of Wyndham. The reef must have been close to the coast, or to a river bank, to allow the mined ore to be carried aboard the vessel on the backs of the crew. Moreover, since Ibrahim would have neither the gear nor the time to permit the sinking of deep shafts, it seems that the outcrop would be portion of a surface one.

In the early years of this century an Englishman named Lang in the employ of Ibrahim's great grandson learned the story of the lost reef. He made frequent visits to the north west in search of it and became well known in those parts. Eventually the search became such an obsession with him that he ended his days there and was last seen in 1939 travelling with a treacherous tribe of wild natives in the Kimberley country.

An interesting angle to the story concerns a hatter, known only as Mad Jack, who for more than twenty years frequented the coastal country between Broome and Wyndham. About twice a year he would put into either of those ports in his small cutter, load up with provisions, and sail away, alone.

Early in 1909 the cutter was found moored in a tidal creek near Yampi Sound. On her deck lay Mad Jack's body with several spear holes through it and the head split open with a tomahawk. In the cabin were a few ounces of alluvial gold and a kerosene tin full of rich silver ore.

Had Mad Jack stumbled on the lost silver reef? If so, the secret died with him.

THE WILD COLONIAL BOYS

First Bushrangers; Ned Kelly; Thunderbolt; Matthew Brady;
Captain Melville; Captain Moonlight; Jackey Jackey;
The Bushrangers' Holiday; 'King of the Bushrangers'.

FIRST BUSHRANGERS
The name 'bushranger' explains itself and was the term given by the
authorities to those who engaged in robbery under arms. From the
desperate exploits of Michael Howe in the early days of Tasmania, to
the reign of terror by the Kelly gang in the late seventies of last century

75

bushranging was a disreputable phase of Australian history which has long since been relegated to the past.

The first bushrangers were escaped convicts who had to rob to live. Starvation or robbery was their choice and they would rather die than return to manacles and chains. Later, when the goldfields were yielding their rich treasures, free men of the more adventurous type were tempted by the opportunities offered by attacking and robbing the gold convoys on their way from the diggings to the coast.

NED KELLY

Mention bushrangers to most Australians anywhere, and they will talk of the Kelly gang. Ned Kelly has become almost a legendary figure: many stories concerning him are widely believed, while many people regard him as a hero who took to bushranging only because he was wronged, and persecuted by the police. Books, articles, plays, even a ballet have been devoted to Kelly and his gang. Fiction has been liberally mingled with fact by many writers.

In his introduction to *Ned Kelly: Being His Own Story of His Life and Crimes*, Clive Turnbull describes the notorious outlaw as our only folk hero, truly observing that the phrase 'Game as Ned Kelly' has become part of the national idiom.

Other writers consider (and with much justification on the evidence of contemporary accounts), that the most notorious of all bushrangers was a hardened scoundrel, neither chivalrous nor brave.

Glenrowan and neighbouring districts will always be known as the 'Kelly Country'. When their daring, swift, mysterious movements and their ruthlessness kept the residents of Glenrowan and other little Victorian townships in a state of alarm, Ned Kelly and his companions in crime had many friends besides their own near relatives. Indeed, their sympathisers were legion throughout Australia. After the gang had been broken up, certain papers and documents were found which indicated that Ned went close to altering the whole political history of Victoria. It is said that he intended proclaiming north-eastern Victoria a Republic with Benalla the capital city and himself as President.

Around the campfire, in the old colonial days, yarns of bushranging exploits were favourite topics of the drovers, shearers and station hands. Here are some of these stories:

THUNDERBOLT

Fred Ward, better known as 'Thunderbolt', was the last of the bushrangers in New South Wales. He commenced his reign in 1863, holding up coach after coach. But he never used violence. Many were his daring robberies, and always this handsome outlaw would ride away with his plunder, singing at the top of his voice. Although wanted dead or alive (and he was finally shot down in 1870) the troubadour bushranger inspired none of the terror caused by some of the early outlaws. Indeed his exploits were taken good-humouredly by most people, for he had lots of friends and admirers.

A tale is told that Thunderbolt held up a German brass band while the musicians were rehearsing in the district of Goonoo Goonoo, on their way to the town of Tenterfield. When the conductor of the band protested that they would be stranded without the few pounds that they possessed, Thunderbolt said he was sorry but that he wanted to put the money on a 'dead cert' at the Tenterfield races the following day. He added, however, that if the horse won he would return the money in care of the Tenterfield post-office. Thunderbolt's horse won his race, and the money was returned to the German band.

On one occasion Thunderbolt rode up to Tabulam Station, on the Clarence River. He was picturesquely dressed in a cabbage-tree hat, moleskins, and a blue shirt. Nearing the homestead he dismounted and tied up his magnificent horse. The lady of the household was not unduly alarmed at the sight of the handsome stranger, who flourished his hat and asked politely, 'May I crave a glass of water?' She fetched him the water and, as he drank, he remarked casually, 'You are alone, I presume?' 'Yes', she answered, guilelessly. The gallant stranger then blew a whistle and two other men appeared from nowhere. The lady was wearing a beautiful enamelled watch suspended round her neck. (This watch was given at her death to the Sydney Art Gallery.) When Thunderbolt demanded it she said that it had belonged to her dear mother and was the only keepsake she had of her. 'You can keep it,' Thunderbolt replied, 'but lead us over the house. We want all the money and valuables you have.'

As the owner of the house had taken everything of value into Casino that morning, the lady did not mind showing them over the place, where they found nothing to their purpose. As they passed one of the bedrooms she turned to Thunderbolt, saying, 'Will you please tell them to walk on tiptoe past this door? My sister is ill and must not be disturbed.' Then followed the strange sight of the crinolined lady with three bushrangers in her wake all walking on tiptoe.

Matthew Brady

The Tasmanian outlaw, Matthew Brady, was a spirited youth of good education who was transported to Van Diemen's Land for forgery. When he turned bushranger he soon earned the nickname of 'Gentleman Brady'. On one occasion, when he held up the Duke of York Inn, he saw an officer whom he mistook for Colonel Balfour, notorious for his ill-treatment of convicts. Brady knocked the man down, but on learning that it was not Colonel Balfour he offered a flowery apology and tried to console his victim.

With three of his gang Brady raided the residence of the Rev Dr Browne, of Launceston. The minister was sitting with his wife, who had been confined only a few hours before. He begged them not to make a disturbance that might alarm Mrs Browne. The bushrangers appeared greatly concerned, apologised for coming at such a time, and promised to be very quiet. The promise was so faithfully kept that Mrs Browne's sister, in a nearby room, was not aware of the visit until next morning. The gentlemen of the road took all available cash and goods!

It seems that Matthew Brady was always considerate to women. One time when he raided a house, and was surprised by the troopers, he took great pains to see that the ladies there would not be injured by the firing. Then there was the instance concerning Mrs Beckford, wife of the organist of St John's Church, Launceston. Their home was on the banks of the Tamar, thirteen miles from the township. One day Mrs Beckford was alone, hanging out the washing, when she was startled by the report of a gun. Brady walked over to her, saying: 'Forgive me, my dear lady, for frightening you, but I just killed that native in time. I happened to be passing through the bush when I caught sight of him with poised spear. As you were working, unconscious of your peril, he was just about to throw the spear at you.'

Mrs Beckford, grateful beyond measure, although she knew her deliverer was the notorious outlaw, invited him to her home and replenished his stores with provisions and foodstuffs from her well-stocked pantry. This, despite the fact that it was a very serious crime to assist a bushranger in any way.

Another daring episode was the raiding of the home of Mr Cruttenden in the district of Sorrell by Brady and his gang. They made the owner a prisoner, together with his servants. Now it happened that Mr Cruttenden was expecting a party of friends from Hobart to dine with him. When these people arrived, later in the day, they were received at the door by Brady, whom they did not know, and naturally thought was a friend of their host. Imagine their consternation when they were shown into the room and saw Mr Cruttenden and his servants tied up! Before they could do a thing the bushrangers had them trussed up, also. Then the outlaws sat down to the table and feasted themselves on the grand dinner prepared for the guests, whilst those poor people could only look on helplessly.

But that was not all. When it was getting dusk, Brady and his gang left the house, leaving their prisoners still tied up. The bushrangers then made their way into the township of Sorrell and went straight to the jail. Arriving there they found a group of soldiers cleaning their muskets. In a jiffy they had the soldiers secured, and, taking them into the jail, locked them up, at the same time releasing all the prisoners. Then they made off to their mountain hide-out.

When Governor Sir George Arthur dispatched all his forces to capture Brady dead or alive, the daring outlaw showed his contempt by posting large notices in Hobart reading as follows:

Mountain Home. April 25. It has caused Matthew Brady much concern that such a person known as Sir George Arthur is at large. Twenty gallons [75 litres] of rum will be given to any one that will deliver his person to me.

(Signed) MATTHEW BRADY.

Nevertheless Brady's brave days were drawing to a close. Constantly harassed by pursuing troopers, he was separated from his fellow rogues by a shot in his ankle. No longer the proud and chivalrous 'Prince of Bushrangers', Brady was now the anxious and suffering fugitive.

The man who finally ran him to earth was John Batman, who was later to win much greater fame as the founder of the Port Phillip colony. Batman, who migrated from New South Wales to Tasmania, was an expert bushman and experienced explorer. Hearing that Brady had made his retreat in the Western Tier, Batman set out for that wild and rugged country.

On the greenstone slopes of Dry's Bluff, which rises abruptly from the surrounding terrain to some 4,000 feet (1,220 metres), Batman eventually glimpsed his quarry limping slowly, and evidently in pain. At the same moment Brady saw his pursuer. Instantly his dejected look vanished; the gun was at his shoulder, a finger on the trigger. In a firm voice he called out, 'Stand, soldier!'

'I'm no soldier, Brady,' was the reply. 'I'm John Batman; surrender—there is no chance for you.'

The bushranger waited a few moments before replying, 'You are right, Batman; my time is come. I yield to you because you're a brave man.'

Petitions poured in to the governor to save Brady from the gallows. Settlers told of his forbearance and women of his kindness. His cell table was loaded with presents of wine, fruit, flowers and cakes sent by his admirers. A dense mass of spectators watched his execution in Hobart; the men cheered him for his courage and women wept for the man who died more like a martyr than a felon.

CAPTAIN MELVILLE

Worthy of a Hollywood movie is the episode of Captain Melville—the Beau Brummel of bushrangers—paying his unexpected visit to the homestead of the wealthy Victorian squatter, McKinnon.

Young and handsome, and extremely fond of dress, Melville surprised the household just as Mr McKinnon and his two attractive daughters were leaving for a country ball. He ordered everyone into the drawing-room: 'Sit down, everybody! My deepest apologies to you Mr McKinnon, and your household, for this unusual intrusion, but I feel in the mood for a little musical relaxation.

'I understand that you and your two charming daughters are very excellent musicians. I, myself, am an ardent music lover but, unfortunately, my occupation gives me little opportunity to indulge in such luxury. Hence this visit.

'My "desires" are usually fulfilled, and I have no doubt they will be on this occasion. Come, now! Don't look so uncomfortable! Let's spend a pleasant musical evening ....'

Too helpless to do otherwise, Mr McKinnon 'obliged'. His daughters played the piano and sang duets. The bushranger later went to the grand piano and placing his gun on the music stand sang a group of Moore's Irish melodies. He also revealed himself as a talented solo pianist.

The evening went on in this amazing fashion when suddenly, in answer to a call for help from one of the servants, mounted police arrived. But Melville got away. Leaping through a window the bushranger made good his escape.

CAPTAIN MOONLIGHT

Beneath the garb of a clergyman beat the heart of a rogue who became one of Australia's legendary bushrangers —Captain Moonlight.

George Scott was a lay preacher in Victoria who deserted the path of Holy Writ and took to the pathless bush. He came from New Zealand, and being a man of good education found employment as a lay reader in the Anglican church at Egerton, a small town between Geelong and Ballarat. It was not long before he became the darling of the parish and the whitehaired boy of the Melbourne diocese.

One night, Mr Prothero, the manager of the Union Bank at Egerton, was stretched out in an easy chair in his comfortable room on the bank premises, warming his feet. A glass of whisky, convenient to his hand, showed that he was warming himself within as well as without. Hearing the door open, Prothero looked around. What he saw surprised and amused him: no other than the Reverend George Scott, clerically garbed, reversed collar and all. But for some extraordinary reason he was masked.

'What's the joke, man?' exclaimed Prothero, 'Good gracious, what's the joke? Are you going to a masked ball? Hey! What are you doing at that drawer? My—my revolver! Confound you, Scott, don't you dare point that revolver at me! It's loaded! What the devil's the matter with you? Have you lost your reason?'

'The mistake you're making, Prothero,' said Scott, 'is that you think I'm joking. I'm not! You're well aware that there's a bullet in the barrel of this gun. Step over to this table—now write on this sheet of paper what I dictate—"CAPTAIN MOONLIGHT HAS ROBBED ME AND STUCK UP THE BANK." Now sign it—"WILLIAM PROTHERO." Leave the note in the middle of the desk—there. Now, Prothero, you will walk in front of me to the bank chamber. And remember—if you make one false move it will be your last move!'

Had Prothero turned round whilst he was writing he would have seen his captor flick open the lid protecting the face of the eight-day clock on the mantel-shelf and push the minute hand on thirty minutes. As they left the room he heard the clock strike ten.

In the bank chamber notes and gold to the value of a couple of thousand pounds were handed over to the menacing visitor who then quickly bound and gagged his captor.

That same night in the parlour of the local pub a number of the townspeople were gathered as was their custom after the day's work.

The Reverend Mr Scott strolled in and with a cheery greeting to all in general said that he was looking for old Danny Richards as he was anxious for him to do a small repair job in the church. Richards not being around he bade them all good night. As an afterthought he asked the time, and being told that it was a quarter-to-ten remarked that he did not realise the hour was so late.

Shortly after ten a man named Thomas, a friend of the bank manager, came rushing into the parlour, waving the note from Prothero's desk and calling loudly for the police.

Next day Prothero was interrogated by a police inspector:

'I tell you, Inspector, it was Scott—the *"Reverend"* Mr Scott! There was NO Captain Moonlight, or any other such person! Scott forced me to write the name "Captain Moonlight".'

'Mr Prothero, I can well understand you being robbed by a masked man dressed as a clergyman, but surely you must be mistaken in thinking it was the Reverend George Scott! It's fantastic!'

When Prothero maintained that the robber was Scott the inspector demanded, 'Then answer me this! You say that he marched you to the bank chamber at ten o'clock—that you heard the hour strike and that your clock is a reliable one. There are witnesses to swear that at a quarter to ten the Reverend Scott was in the parlour of the hotel looking for old Mr Richards. Indeed, he had just left there when your friend, Thomas—I repeat *your friend*—came running there with the news of the alleged hold-up!'

Needless to say, Parson Scott professed to be appalled by the terrible charge laid against him. What is more, he had everybody's sympathy. Prothero and his friend were not believed. They were both arrested. £2,000 had disappeared from the bank and both men were called upon to find sureties and personal guarantees to come up for trial if called.

Soon afterwards Mr Scott discreetly left the district. A few years later the city of Sydney was graced with the presence of a distinguished visitor who was entertained by high society until he gave a bad cheque for the purchase of a luxury yacht. It was his turn now to be arrested. The police discovered that this elegant trickster had once been a preacher in the Victorian town of Egerton, where he was known by the name of Scott. Messrs Prothero and Thomas were immediately cleared of the charges laid against them, and Scott was given ten years imprisonment.

From then onwards, George Scott, reverend or not, was known colloquially as Captain Moonlight. As such, after graduation from prison, he took to the road and with his gang led the famous raid on Wantabadgery, vieing for notoriety with Ned Kelly. The clerical Captain made his final bow to the world on the gallows at Darlinghurst.

JACKEY JACKEY

Among Australian bushrangers none struck the public imagination of his day more than William John Westwood, better known as 'Jackey Jackey—the gentleman bushranger'. The nickname 'Jackey Jackey' was given him after a brave and noble Red Indian Chief then in the world's eye.

Westwood had a reputation for good manners, consideration for women and innocence of bloodshed. He was born in 1820, the son of an English farmer in Kent. He was well educated but at the age of sixteen was found guilty of forgery and transported to Botany Bay as a convict. On the farm where he worked the overseer was far too fond of the lash, so, three years later, at the age of twenty, Westwood escaped and took to the bush.

Many colourful tales are told of the escapades of this handsome highwayman. One concerns a Grand Ball in Sydney given by Governor Gipps in 1841. The parliamentary member for Parramatta was on his way to the function when he was bailed up by Westwood:

'You may put your hands down, Mr Gorman. I'm not going to rob you. I merely wish to accompany you to the Governor's Ball this evening. I want you to take me along as your friend.

'Now don't look so astonished. You can see that under my cloak I'm dressed the part—full evening clothes. All you have to do is to introduce me as an English friend, recently arrived here.'

'Are you crazy, man!' exclaimed Gorman. 'Are you trying to stage a hold-up there? You must know that there will be police and a military guard!'

'My dear sir, I'm not going to rob anyone at the Ball, I assure you, though I may steal the heart of some fair damsel. I'll be a thorough gentleman. But mark you this—if you warn anyone of my identity I'll shoot to kill!'

Westwood not only attended the Ball but was introduced to the Governor and members of the Vice-Regal party. Despite the flutter of excitement he caused among the ladies the young stranger disappeared as mysteriously as he came. Even the Honourable Member for Parramatta seemed strangely silent about his vanished friend.

Another of Westwood's escapades was his cool daring in making an appearance at a billiard saloon in the town of Goulburn when all the troopers were after him. Dressed like a shearer, and pretending to be a little drunk, he approached three of the local billiards experts and challenged them to a game. Producing a wad of notes he offered to play all three for £100 stakes. After beating them hands down he collected the money, shouted drinks all round, announced his identity and withdrew unmolested.

Eventually when captured, Westwood was imprisoned on Cockatoo Island. Here he organised a mass escape, and led it by swimming from the island to the Balmain shore—a distance of about 440 yards (402 metres) through shark-infested waters. Captured again, he was sent to the dreaded Port Arthur penal settlement in Tasmania. He was only twenty-two, and so far had not inflicted bodily harm on anyone. Here he witnessed for the first time the torturing of prisoners and the inhuman treatment by many of the warders. His only friend was the chaplain who was powerless to help him.

Finally, unable to stand the treatment any longer, he decided to end it all. Calling together some of the other convicts he addressed them as follows: 'I've made up my mind to stand this oppression no longer. I'm making an escape—though I'm certain to be caught. And that means the gallows. Yet death will be preferable to this hell. If any of you wish to follow me—you know what your fate will be!'

Led by Westwood a number of the convicts made the break. All were caught and sentenced to death. Just before his execution Westwood wrote a letter to the prison chaplain at Port Arthur. That letter is still preserved. In it he thanks the chaplain for his many acts of kindness, but it concludes with these words: My grave will be a haven. Flogged, goaded and tantalised, I have been reduced to a lunatic and savage. Out of my bitter cup of sorrow the sweetest draught is that which takes away the misery of living death.

The Bushrangers' Holiday

Many of the bushrangers were thoroughly bad lots, committing crimes as callously as a tiger kills its prey. But there were others who avoided bloodshed and acted almost in the Robin Hood manner—when their victims made no resistance.

Some of the bushranging furnished dramatic situations stronger,

more stirring and realistic than much that is found in romantic novels. Much, too, of the bushranging had its humorous side.

One of the drollest stories concerns the well-known New South Wales bushrangers, Ben Hall, Johnny Gilbert and John O'Meally. One day in 1862 this trio, perhaps out of sheer boredom, decided to have a holiday. At any rate, early on this particular morning Mr Robinson, the licensee of the hotel at the small township of Canowindra, was awakened by loud knocking. From his bedroom he called out:

'Go away! Go away! We're full up! It's no use knocking there's no room here!'

'It's the police!' came the rejoinder. 'Open up in the name of the Law! And be quick about it!'

The publican quickly got out of bed, hurried to the front door and unlocked it. When he saw the visitors he cried out angrily:

'You—you lying hounds! How dare you tell me you're the police! Get to the devil you—'

'Take it steady—take it steady, my man,' answered the spokesman. 'You should fear us more than the police. Here I'll step nearer the light where you can see my face.'

The publican cried out in dread, 'Hall—Ben Hall!'

'Correct. Allow me to introduce my two friends—Johnny Gilbert and John O'Meally.'

Rallying from his fright the publican began to bluster. 'You're wasting your time here. I banked all the takings yesterday. There's no more than three quid in the bar.' Ben Hall laughed good-humouredly.

'We're not here to take your money, but to give you ours. We'd like to have a few days' holiday here. A bit of social life—a little relaxation—some music and good food.' The publican stared at him in amazement.

'What are you talking about? Don't be crazy! There are more than a dozen people staying here. Some of them will know you, and there'll be customers coming and going who are sure to recognise you.'

Ben Hall had a ready answer for that one. 'There may be customers coming—but they won't be going. At least they won't be leaving until we finish our holiday. They'll just have to stay and join in the fun!'

'You surely don't think you can take charge of this pub and hold captive guests and customers while you go on a spree!' Mr Robinson expostulated.

'Spree? My dear Mr Robinson, we're not here for a drunken orgy. You'll find during the three days we intend spending here that we'll be perfect gentlemen.' The bushranger drew himself up arrogantly. 'But we're wasting time,' he continued.

'Please ring the bell and assemble your guests in the dining-room.'

'But it's so early! Look here—' protested Mr Robinson.

'Get moving! You heard the order!' came the curt command.

When the bewildered guests were brought to the dining room Ben Hall addressed them:

'Our humble apologies for all this inconvenience. This little gathering will increase in numbers with new arrivals during the next few days. As a matter of fact we propose to assemble all the township here.' He looked keenly at the startled assemblage and went on coolly:

'No doubt you're already aware of my identity and that of my two friends. But you've nothing to fear. We've come here simply for a three-day holiday and we want everyone, young and old, to have a good time. Let's have songs, games, and plenty of fun! Drinks will be on the house, but there'll be no drunkenness. The women and children can be assured that horse-play won't be tolerated.

'To anyone who might try to alter my plans I would like to inform them that I have scouts posted outside the town to keep a close watch on everything.' Then he turned to address the publican's wife who was listening with her mouth open in amazement.

'Oh—Mrs Robinson! See to it that everyone has a first-class breakfast to begin the day. We want all the meals to be extra special. This must be a holiday that we'll remember with pleasure! Thank you everybody.'

It was a worried publican who later in the day approached Ben Hall, exclaiming:

'You'll ruin me! Look what it will cost me for the brandy and cigars you've ordered for the men! And the sweets for the women and kids!'

'Must I tell you again,' replied Hall, 'that this is *my* party? I've brought a wad of notes that will more than pay for everything.'

They both looked at the door as O'Meally walked into the room calling out: 'Hey, Ben! Johnny and I marched the copper down here! He's the only one in the town. We've got him on the verandah.'

'Bring the poor coot into the dining-room,' advised Hall, 'and let him join the company. What about the rest of the town mob?'

'We've got 'em rounded up. There's about forty in the pub now.'

'What about customers?' Ben wanted to know.

'There's not been many, so far—just a few bullockies. They'd been camping the night outside the town. And were they surprised when they strolled into the bar! Their eyes nearly popped out when they saw the muster!' O'Meally grinned. 'But they didn't mind when they found it was a free-for-all party!'

'It's been a mad day, all right! I think, though, that most of them are having a good time,' said Ben with satisfaction.

'My oath they are!' O'Meally declared, laughing. 'One bloke said to me, "You bushies can keep up this party for as long as you like, as far as I'm concerned!" '

With a hearty laugh Hall exclaimed, 'It was a bit slow in the beginning trying to get everyone to look happy, but they soon warmed up. Tonight it should be better. I'm getting old mum Robinson to serve roast turkey and all the trimmings for dinner.' The captive guests included an old drover with a concertina who squeezed out many a lively tune and sentimental ballad for the community sing-songs.

Two bullockies who complained that their stock would be thirsty were allowed to go out and water them under the watchful eye of one of the bushrangers. Early on the third day a man came to Hall and said that he was enjoying himself so much he didn't want to leave but because flood waters were making the creek rise it was imperative for him to get his buggy across, otherwise he might be prevented from returning home for a month. He was allowed to go.

At bed time the women and children were allowed to go to their rooms but the men had to sit round the big dining table with their hands in view. The only way they could sleep was by resting their hands on the table. The bushrangers took short naps in turn while one remained on guard. Whether they had sentries posted outside the little township, as they said, is doubtful. Probably it was merely bluff.

At sunset on the third day of their holiday the bushrangers made their departure. For sixty hours they had held captive everyone, including the policeman, in the little bush town.

But they left no ill-feelings behind them. They paid the final reckoning for the party (and it amounted to no small sum), then gravely thanked those assembled company for their attendance. And so the incredible holiday came to an end.

The three young outlaws rode off on their horses—fine thorough-breds stolen from rich squatters—waving gaily at the crowd on the verandah, who waved back with cheers and shouts of good wishes!

Perhaps this legendary tale has been embellished down the years—as so often happens with folk-lore—but certainly the incident of the three bushrangers holding the little township (including the policeman) captive in the hotel for three days is authentic history.

KING OF THE BUSHRANGERS

It's worth recording that in the bushranging days country people did not take their pleasures sadly. They were not unduly alarmed about the activities of the hold-up men, and indeed were wont to treat such matters lightly. It was the city folk who did the worrying—probably as the result of the terrifying tales about the bush bandits that daily appeared in their newspapers.

In those days nothing gave greater fun to the country dwellers than the successful 'taking down' of chappies from the city. They lost no opportunity in endeavouring to do so when any of the 'townies' came among them on business or on pleasure bent.

So it was that this incident took place. It was during the time when the notorious bushranger Frank Gardiner was King of the Road in New South Wales. The location was Muswellbrook. A Sydney reporter happened to put up at one of the hotels there. Staying at the

same hostelry were three young men of the district much given to practical joking. Having taken the measure of the city visitor they proceeded to victimise him in a manner that was certainly original. They began it all by engaging him in conversation....

'Yes, I'm a Sydney journalist, you know. I've just come from Scone. My paper sent me there to report on the opening of the new Town Hall there. All very boring. What a sleepy hollow this place is. Does anything ever happen around these parts?' he asked in a superior manner.

'Can't say it does, much,' said the first joker, 'except, of course, when the bushrangers get busy.'

'They must be a great trial to you country folk. By jove, they seem to be making their presence felt, from all accounts. Tell me—have you ever encountered one of these gentlemen of the road ?'

'My oath! But some of 'em are pretty decent coves. And that goes for Frank Gardiner. Why, my two mates here and myself happen to know Frank personally.'

'Frank Gardiner—King of the Bushrangers?' the reporter asked incredulously.

'As a matter of fact,' answered another of the trio in a confidential tone, 'Gardiner is camped just outside this very town.'

'You don't say so! Frank Gardiner right here!' The jokers exchanged a sly wink.

'Sh! Sh! Not so loud! I'm telling you this in confidence,' one of them said in a guarded whisper.

'Sorry, old man, but I'm so interested in all this. Here—let's have a drink. The shout's on me. Waiter! Four beers, please.' The reporter's 'nose for news' twitched expectantly.

'Yes,' said the first joker, 'what Bill said is true. Gardiner is no more that a mile away from this pub.'

The young man felt he was on a scoop. 'Maybe it would be a good idea for me to stay here for another day or two,' he suggested hopefully. 'He may be contemplating a raid somewhere in the town and I'd be on the spot to write-up an eyewitness account.'

'No—I don't think so,' remarked another of the men.

'Gardiner keeps away from town jobs.'

'A pity,' said the reporter, 'I mean as far as my getting a newspaper story. One has to be always on one's toes in my profession, you know. It's a case of quick thinking and smart work.'

'Look here, mate,' said the first joker, 'You seem a fair dinkum bloke, and I know my two cobbers here will agree with me when I suggest that we may be able to do something for you. I think we could arrange to give you an introduction to Gardiner. You could interview him for your newspaper.'

'But—you surely can't mean it!' the other exclaimed, his eyes fairly goggling. 'In any case I shouldn't think he'd care for that sort of thing!'

'Oh, wouldn't he!' was the airy answer. 'That's just the very thing he'd fancy! If you say the word we'll get in touch with him and arrange a meeting.'

'Jove! What a story an interview with Gardiner would make! Well, I'm on fast enough!' Then with a cautiousness that made the jokers laugh, he added nervously, 'Do you think there'd be much—er— danger? I mean one's personal safety kind of thing?'

'Don't worry—Gardiner won't harm you. This will be strictly a social visit,' he was assured.

'But we better be off at once to make arrangements. We'll let you know before dark. Mum's the word! Don't open your lips about it to a soul—if you value your life. You've got to bear in mind that we're running some risk.'

And so the plotters left the pressman to conjure up rosy visions of fame as the journalist who scooped the most sensational interview of the day.

When darkness had fully set in two of the three friends reappeared at the hotel. The reporter hurried to them, exclaiming:

'Did you manage it? Did he say he—'

'Sh! Sh!' whispered one joker, 'Damn it, man, don't speak aloud or you'll spoil everything. As it is, old Kelly the publican looks as if he smells a rat. That's why Jack didn't return with us. We mustn't act suspiciously.'

'Sorry, old chap. It's just my eagerness.' The reporter was apologetic.

'Well, everything is set,' the joker said secretively, 'but we must be careful that no one here follows us. We'll move over to the bar and have another drink. I'll suggest a walk before we turn into bed; then you can pipe up and say you think you'll join us.'

Sauntering from the hotel the trio made their way to the outskirts of the town. The reporter's excitement increased perceptibly as one of his companions whispered suddenly:

'There—through the trees—there's the hut! And now we have to watch our step. Gardiner arranged a signal for us. I have to whistle a few bars of "The Dear Little Shamrock" as we approach.'

Whistling the Irish tune the leader walked to the door and knocked. From within came a voice calling out: 'Who is it?'

'Friends, with a visitor, as arranged,' answered the whistler.

'Enter quickly and without noise!'

A bolt was withdrawn, the door opened, and when the three men walked in, the door was immediately shut and bolted again.

The hut was meagrely furnished; a table on which stood a lighted candle stuck in a bottle, a small box or two evidently arranged as seats, and a few cooking utensils and articles of crockery. But the pressman had no eye for surroundings, his whole attention being taken up with observation of the central figure seated at the table, and who was at once introduced to him as Gardiner.

And, of a truth, he saw something worth looking at. The 'King of the Bushrangers' was dressed in a style worthy of that title. He wore leather boots reaching to his thighs, turned-up collar, panama hat jauntily cocked on one side, corduroy trousers, and a grey tunic edged with red. Around his waist was buckled a large leather belt containing no less than four revolvers, a bowie knife, a whisky flask, a long German pipe and white leather gauntlet gloves. His whole appearance was that of a brigand ready for active work.

The pressman's experience in the journalistic world had not schooled him to absolute fearlessness. Indeed, he showed marked signs of timidity as the notorious bushranger confronted him with a look indicative of annoyance or anger and asked in arrogant tones what it was that his visitor wished to see him about.

As the reporter meekly indicated that he simply wished for an interview for press purposes and that he would be pleased to convey any message from Gardiner to the general public, and give him a chance to express his views on any subject, the bushranger's manner thawed. He entered into a general conversation with his visitor, of whom he had this to say:

'I must admit you have more than a spark of pluck to venture into my temporary hiding-place. And I admire you for it. As a gentleman of the road I salute you as a gentleman of the press!

'Not that I have any liking for the press! Why, blast my eyes, man, the press have been hounding me right from the beginning! They've circulated false reports about me—charged me with every petty robbery committed! They must have known it was impossible for me to flit from place to place in the time unless I had wings. And I'm not an angel yet! Ha! Ha! Ha!

'What's more, I'll have it known that I despise petty thieves! I engage only in major operations! Any more questions?'

Hesitantly, the reporter answered:

'Er—would you care to air your views on the Police Department, or on the—er—Chief of Police, Sir Frederick Pottinger?'

'Sir Frederick! The man who's sworn to capture me in person! Let me tell you that the Chief of Police is nothing but a nincompoop! An idle boaster! If I come across Sir Frederick I'll horsewhip him soundly—I wouldn't condescend to shoot such a louse! Put that in your paper in capital letters!' He paused for a moment and suddenly exclaimed:

'Holy Moses! What's the time?'

'Er—pardon?' said the reporter, taken aback.

'The time! The time! What's the time?'

'Oh—it's nearly ten o'clock,' he replied, looking at his watch.

'Hm. I'll just make it nicely.' Then addressing all in general he said:

'Gentlemen—this evening you'll be privileged to see me in action. I've had reliable information to the effect that a stockowner will be passing along the road near this hut soon after ten o'clock. He's coming from Maitland, after selling a mob of cattle there. Five hundred head. His purse should be a heavy one. The three of you may accompany me.'

In a terrified voice the pressman exclaimed: 'I-I'd rather not! I'll stay in the hut! No—no—I'll hurry back to town.'

The bushranger regarded him sternly.

'No one is to make for town until I've completed my job. And the hut is to be locked up. I'm leaving for a new hide-out.'

'But don't you see the risk I'm running—breaking the law? After all, there might be—' the reporter pleaded.

'Shut up! You heard my orders!' was the brusque response.

One of the jokers whispered to the journalist:

'You've nothing to worry about, mate. Frank will see that we're in no danger. In any case, your part in the hold-up will never be known! We'll keep mum! And think of the thrilling story you'll be able to give in your newspaper of how Gardiner conducts operations!'

'Come on, quickly!' ordered Gardiner. 'Keep close to me and move very quietly.'

It was a case of Hobson's choice. The pressman, half bewildered at the turn affairs had taken, resigned himself to the inevitable. The bushranger posted the two friends behind a convenient bush, but insisted that the gentleman of the press stay by his side.

Presently there came the sound of a rider coming leisurely down the road. As he came into view round the bend, Gardiner levelled a revolver and commanded: 'Bail up! Get down from that horse!'

'By thunder I can't get down quick enough!' the rider yelled back.

The reporter gaped in astonishment as the pseudo Gardiner turned on his heels and ran off; but before he could gather his wits the rider was facing him menacingly.

'Ho! So your white-livered mate's left you! Run off like a stinking dingo! Well, by cripes, I've got *you*. And *you're* not getting away!' Here he suited action to words.

'Let me go—let me go!'

'I'll belt the daylights out of you! We've had enough of you yellow-bellied reptiles disturbing the peace of the countryside! I'm going to take the law into my own hands! I'm going to bash your brains out here and now!'

'For pity's sake—I beg of you to listen to me! I was forced into this! I—'

'*Forced* into highway robbery! You're a liar as well as a thief! I'll—'

'You're choking the life out of me! The man who ran away was Frank Gardiner. He—'

'So you're one of Gardiner's gang! That settles it! I'll murder—'

'For mercy's sake—listen to me—what—what's the matter?…'

The 'stockowner' had suddenly collapsed with helpless laughter. The laughter was taken up, swelled out, and continued by three others who came from behind some thick bushes—'Gardiner' and the other two rascals who had played upon the susceptibilities of the journalist. However, he was too relieved to reproach them. To the echoes of their laughter he returned to the pub, a sorer, sadder, wiser man.

UNUSUAL CHARACTERS

*The King of the Hawkesbury; A Picturesque Pioneer; Queen of Scotland
Island; Margaret Catchpole; One of the Old Breed; Francis Morgan;
Good King Joe; Quong Tart; Amazon of the Manning River;
A Mass Murderer; A Woman Pirate; The Eliza Emily Donnithorne
Legend; The Elulo Queen; Christy Palmerston; Dr Robinson;
The Magpie; The Man Who Saw a Unicorn; Captain Piper;
Granny Smith and Her Famous Apple.*

THE KING OF THE HAWKESBURY

There are not many more beautiful places in New South Wales than
the spot where the old Northern Road crosses the Hawkesbury River

at Wiseman's Ferry, some 52 miles (84 kilometres) from Sydney. For many years it was an important station on the land route between the capital and the Hunter Valley.

Solomon Wiseman, the man who gave his name to the ferry, must have possessed some remarkable qualities. He came to the colony because he could not see eye-to-eye with certain customs men in the Isle of Wight regarding the nocturnal landing of dutiable goods. After serving his sentence of transportation he settled on the Hawkesbury at this spot, long before the road was made. Here he established the first ferry over the river, and it remained the only one for many years. To construct the roadway up the mountains on either side, large numbers of convicts were sent to the ferry, and Solomon Wiseman was appointed District Superintendent. This was a job of some importance, with much power and glory appertaining to it. There were also perquisites of which the astute Solomon was not slow to avail himself.

He supplied provisions to convicts on the Hawkesbury, thereby netting £4,000 a year, and he ruled the whole district. There is a cave on the northern side of the river, known as the Judgment Cave, where Solomon is supposed to have sat and delivered judgment.

There are about twenty houses today in the village of Wiseman's Ferry—or Wiseman's, as it is called locally. The homestead of the King of the Hawkesbury is now an hotel. The original portion of this fine old building has walls about 3 feet (1 metre) thick. He built his house—as all pioneers did—with a view to its lasting. It is two-storeyed with magnificent circular steps leading up to the front verandah.

Legend has it that Solomon used to throw his wives over the balcony on to those steps. Legend gives him three wives, but does not say just how many times he threw each of the ladies over.

But he was a remarkable old man. To quote judge Therry's reminiscences: 'He was quite a character—a person of great natural shrewdness and of considerable prosperity. He was very hospitable, walking round with a telescope under his arm so that he could see his visitors coming from afar. At the time I visited Solomon Wiseman (it was about 1830) he was surrounded by all the substantial comforts that a farmer with a like income enjoys in England. His household consisted of his wife, an amiable Englishwoman, and four sons, remarkably fine youths, varying from thirteen to eighteen years of age. Being inquisitive how these youths were brought up, and how he provided for their education, I found his notions on the subject of education curious and original. He said education was a point on which he was not particular; and asked me what was the good of it? adding the observation that the acquisition of wealth was the main lesson of life. I told him that, amongst other things, "Education aided in the acquirement of property". "Oh," he said, "my views are quite different. I have four sons, and I say to Richard, 'There's a herd of cattle for you', and to Tom 'There's a flock of sheep—look after them.' So, in five years' time they become rich, each the owner of large herds of cattle and flocks of sheep. Now that's what I call education, for by it they acquire means to live." It was idle to reason with mine host on the advantage of the observance of duties, and the restraints that education was designed to confer. He looked only to the one point of material gain, and discarded every other consideration. In literary attainments of any kind Solomon was sadly deficient, and took unmerciful liberties with the English language and English history.'

The story goes that Solomon flogged a convict, who died as a result of it. As he expired he cursed Wiseman. 'You will never rest!' he cried.

Years later the vault in which Solomon was buried was broken open. His coffin was smashed and his bones were scattered. Hoodlums kicked the skull of the King of the Hawkesbury in the dust. Later, what remained of his skeleton was buried in the churchyard. Thus his body did not rest. Nor could his spirit. A traveller from Europe visited the inn in the 1880s. He was given Solomon Wiseman's bedroom. He woke up with the horrid feeling that someone was in the room. Someone was. Solomon Wiseman was standing by the window. The visitor could see through him, and with a piercing shriek, he fled from the room.

A Picturesque Pioneer

In the Pittwater district, on the way to Palm Beach, New South Wales, is a locality called Stokes Point. It is named after a fine old pioneer who lived a secluded life on a little promontory across the bay.

Mr Stokes had been transported to this country for being found with a stolen handkerchief in his possession. But to the end of his days he protested his innocence. Often he told the story:

'It was a lovely Spring day in London, and off I went to Hyde Park to enjoy the sunshine. While I was making my way through the crowd at Piccadilly a pickpocket must have planted the handkerchief on me. Maybe he thought he was being watched, and wanted to get rid of it.

'Fortunately the handkerchief was worth only elevenpence. Had it been valued at a shilling or more I would have been hanged. As it was I was sentenced and transported to New South Wales as a convict.'

The conduct of Mr Stokes after his pardon certainly bore witness to his good character. His neatness and tidiness were as impeccable as they were in London where he was a ladies' shoemaker. He was a resplendent sight every Sabbath when he always came from Pittwater to Mona Vale wearing a tightly fitting bottle-green coat with large pearl buttons, an amazing, tall hat and carrying a walking stick that Beau Brummel might have envied. Once, on arrival at Mona Vale in his wonderful raiment, it was pointed out to him that it was Saturday. 'Oh, my goodness!' he replied, 'I'll have to go home and change. The time goes so slow in Pittwater.'

The Queen of Scotland Island

There is very little about Scotland Island to suggest that once it was of considerable importance in the affairs of the young colony of New South Wales. Situated in the southern portion of Pittwater, not far from Sydney, its heavily timbered slopes today, save for the cleared spaces around the houses, would seem to be in almost the same condition as they were more than a century ago.

In the early years of the last century the island was the scene of considerable shipbuilding activity, in addition to being the site of extensive salt-works. Andrew Thompson, a stalwart pioneer of the Windsor district, was the first owner of the island. He gave it its name, in honour of his native Scotland. In the churchyard at Windsor is the grave of Andrew Thompson; the tombstone bears a long eulogy by Governor Macquarie. Thompson had been transported to Australia for setting fire to a hay stack when he was but fifteen years old, thus displaying, perhaps, a singular initiative in revenging himself upon some nasty Farmer Giles. At any rate after he had served his sentence, he proved an honourable and worthy addition to the land to which he was banished.

On the island he built himself his home, established a farm, and carried on a prosperous business for some years, combining ship-building with other interests. When he died in 1810 the *Sydney Gazette* made mention of the launching of a vessel at Scotland Island 'one of the finest ever built in the colony', and named by Andrew Thompson at the laying-down of the keel as the *Geordy*.

After the death of Thompson many attempts were made to sell the island, but for some considerable time no buyer could be found, for its isolated position rendered farming there an unprofitable venture.

For many years the island remained uninhabited; then came a romantic and mysterious person, one Arnbrof Diersknecht, a Belgian. In company with his wife he rebuilt Thompson's cottage and estab-lished himself on the island. The pair were better known as Mr and Mrs Benns, but the latter, throughout the district, was referred to as the 'Queen of Scotland Island'. She was a little dark woman of gentle manners and great kindness of heart, but with a certain regal bearing. Her jewellery befitted her 'royal' title. She wore ornate golden earrings hanging to her shoulders, bracelets, and a magnificent neck-let. Very little was known of the 'Queen' or her consort, but many picturesque tales were told of their past. There is a story that, before Mrs Benn's death, she buried her collection of valuable jewellery somewhere on the island.

Nor is this the only legendary treasure buried on the island. In Governor Macquarie's term of office there was a scarcity of coined money in the colony. To meet the difficulty the governor gave orders that the five-shilling Spanish dollar, the coin then most in use, should be punched. The small central piece so removed (called the 'dump') was made a coin worth fifteenpence; while the remaining portion, known as the 'holey dollar', was made current at the old value of five shillings. A three-legged pot full of holey dollars is said to have been hidden on Scotland Island by two men in a stolen boat full of stolen treasure in Andrew Thompson's time.

MARGARET CATCHPOLE

'I wonder,' the descendant of an early settler remarked, 'if any of the present generation of Australians know how the very early settlers of Sydney interpreted the musical notes of the butcher-bird? My grandfather used to tell many tales about Margaret Catchpole. One was that so many men asked her to marry them that even the butcher-birds began to mock them. If you listen to one of these birds, especially in the early morning in autumn—it is then that the butcher-bird sings his sweetest songs—it requires no stretch of imagination to hear him say:

' "Pretty Margie Catchpole, won't you marry me?"

'My children are so sure that this is what the butcher-birds say that they always call them "Pretty Margie Catchpoles".'

The legends that linger round Margaret Catchpole are many and varied. It is a fact that she gained local fame in her native English village when, as a young girl, she rode bareback one stormy night to fetch a doctor, some miles distant, for the wife of one of the villagers. On another occasion she jumped fully dressed into a river to save the life of a drowning child.

Margaret Catchpole was born in Seven Hills, near Ipswich, Suffolk, in 1762. She became a domestic at £6 a year and keep in the services of a family named Cobbold, in which there were twenty-two children.

She had a young man named Will Laud, a sailor who later turned down his job for the more profitable one of smuggling.

When Will was caught in the act Margaret determined to be near him. Dressing herself in male attire, she took a horse from the stables of her employer and rode to London, a distance of 70 miles (113 kilometres), in eight and a-half hours—no mean achievement. On her arrival she tried to sell the horse, but was arrested and sentenced to seven years in Ipswich jail. When she had served about three years news came to her through the jail grape vine intelligence that her lover, Will Laud, had managed to escape from prison and was in hiding, waiting for her to join him. She waited the opportunity and soon afterwards made a break. Her lover kept her in hiding but the soldiers found her whereabouts and came to arrest her. Will Laud, in attempting to shield her, was killed, and Margaret was sentenced to death—a sentence later commuted to transportation for life.

And so we find her in Australia. There is some doubt as to the exact year she reached here, but Henry Fulton, a former rector of Windsor and Richmond, says that she came out in the transport *Nile*, which arrived in December 1801. Because of the shortage of domestics in the colony Margaret was not sent to the Female Penitentiary at Parramatta but was assigned as cook and laundress to the Commissary Palmer.

Strangely enough she never married—and this in a community where women were at a premium. Credence is thus given to the story that she had sworn to remain faithful to the memory of her lover, Will Laud. Certain it is that one aspirant for her hand was the brilliant young botanist, George Cayley, sent to Australia as a plant-collector by Sir Joseph Banks.

In her middle-age she worked as a nurse and midwife in the Hawkesbury district. Some of Australia's most noted pioneers were assisted into this world by the very capable hands of Margaret Catchpole. When the terrible floods of 1806 devastated the Hawkesbury flats she was a gallant figure in heroic rescue work.

Though she lies buried somewhere in the Richmond Cemetery, her grave is unknown. In the old register of St Peter's Church, near by, is the last record of Margaret Catchpole—the entry of her death, as inscribed in the year 1819, by the Reverend Henry Fulton:

Margaret Catchpole, aged 51 years, came prisoner in the *Nile* in the year 1801. Died May 13th; was buried May 14th, 1819.

FRANCIS MORGAN
Much of the charm of Sydney lies in its beautiful harbour. Peers and poets have proclaimed its glories.

> *Round the sea-world shine the beacons of a thousand ports o' call,*
> *But the harbour lights of Sydney are the grandest of them all.'*

So sang Henry Lawson. A certain British Prime Minister proclaimed Sydney Harbour as 'a paradise of waters'. But one of the first persons who is recorded as having eulogised the beauty of the harbour was a murderer named Francis Morgan. He did so from the foot of the gallows on Pinchgut Island—if tradition be true.

Everyone who has seen Sydney Harbour has noticed Fort Denison, or Pinchgut, as it was called in the early days. For a short while it was used to house refractory convicts, and as these unfortunates were fed on a small weekly ration of bread and water they soon coined for it the title of Pinchgut.

The island has suffered tremendous change in outline since the First Fleet entered the harbour. It was at that time a conical shaped rocky islet, about 80 feet (25 metres) in height, covered with bushes and stunted trees. Governor Phillip christened it Rock Island, a literal translation of its Aboriginal name Mattenwaya. Soon after the inception of the infant colony it was recognised that the shark-infested waters would make Rock Island an ideal spot for the safeguarding of refractory convicts, so accommodation was made there for them.

In 1796 one, Francis Morgan, was condemned to death in connection with the murder of a man on the North Shore. The place chosen for his execution was on this island. At the foot of the gallows he was asked, before the hangman placed the rope over his head, if he had anything to say. The condemned man replied nonchalantly that he did not feel disposed to speak on such a morbid subject as death, nor was he inspired to make a public confession of his sins. He said that the only thing worth mentioning was the superb view of the harbour from his high elevation, and that he was sure there were no waters the world over to compare with it for beauty.

After his execution it was decided to follow the good old British custom of gibbeting malefactors in prominent places as an example of 'Crime does not pay'. Accordingly the body of Morgan was hung in chains at the top of Pinchgut and dangled there for many months.

In 1840, shortly after the transportation of convicts to Australia had ceased, Sir George Gipps, recognising the value of Pinchgut as a site for fortification, and realising that the supply of cheap convict labour must soon cease, began its transformation by razing the rocky formation almost to water-level. The project, however, was not sanctioned by the Home Authorities and the work was abandoned in 1842 when the island had assumed the appearance of a flat area of rubble, only a few feet above the tide, and about an acre in extent. But the position altered in 1854, when Britain and France found themselves at war with

Russia, and Governor Denison decided that Pinchgut should be fortified. By 1857 the present Martello tower and guard rooms were finished, and the impregnability of the fortress was assured by the mounting of modern artillery capable of hitting a very large object at a very short range, if the target sat very still. The name was changed from Pinchgut to Fort Denison in honour of the Governor of the day.

The walls of the fort are 12 feet (3.7 metres) thick at the base and 9 feet (2.8 metres) at the top. The Martello tower—one of the finest of its type still in existence—remains as it was when it formed Sydney's chief defence. The huge blocks of stone are locked together by small coned cross-pieces of granite, revealing true expertness in the stone-mason's art. Narrow stairs wind up to the gun-room where, in perfect order, are three of the old eight-inch 32-pounders.

Many people are under the impression that the cells were used for the imprisonment and torture of manacled prisoners. That is not correct. The cells were used for the storage of powder and shot.

In 1900 the island was taken over by the Harbour Trust, under whose control it still remains.

REIGN OF GOOD KING JOE

His name never appeared in *Who's Who* or any directory, but Robert Joel Cooper, better known in the North as King Joe, was one of the most remarkable and colourful of our pioneers, the only white man ever to become the absolute ruler of a tribe of Aborigines.

King Joe's kingdom was Melville Island, North Australia, and he ruled his subjects firmly for many years. Physically and mentally he was a fine type of Australian, upright and honourable and of commanding appearance. He stood well over 6 feet (180 centimetres) in height and had a remarkably keen pair of blue eyes.

Cooper arrived in the Northern Territory in 1881, having come overland from South Australia, where he was born. Utterly fearless, and straight in all his dealings, he soon won over the fierce Melville Islanders, and before long was proclaimed Chief over the Five Tribes. He was put through all the secret rites of the Aborigines, and to the day of his death never revealed them to another white man.

King Joe was a man who would carry out his principles unswervingly. He was a non-smoker and a teetotaller—an exceedingly rare combination in white men who live in North Australian bush country, far removed from civilisation.

Before he was chosen chief, trouble was always brewing on Melville Island. The islanders were a warlike race, avoided by both whites and blacks.

When Cooper took charge all this was altered. He ruled with a rod of iron, but always justly. The punishment of evil-doers he attended to personally. Wearing only a loincloth, he would take a spear, woomera and throwing-stick, and hunt down any native who had broken one of the tribal laws and had fled to escape punishment. Being a fine tracker, as well as a first-class bushman, he always returned with the offender.

For a white man to be made a chief of wild Aborigines was an honour not easily won. Even when Cooper had been accepted by the tribes, two native pretenders to the 'throne' challenged him to combat. Both were powerful young athletes famed for their prowess as warriors.

Cooper accepted their challenge and prepared for a battle in which he was to fight both men in turn. Surrounded by hundreds of natives, he and his first opponent faced each other. They wore loincloths and carried only spears and a woomera each. They were separated by about 100 yards (91 metres), and at a given signal each began to creep up on the other. The white man had learned to throw spears when quite a lad and was an expert in the art. However, the native knew all the tricks, too. So agile were the pair that this first test ended in a stalemate neither drew blood.

The council of the old men of the tribes then decided that, as both were evenly skilled, they should come to grips with waddies. These weapons are about 6 feet (180 centimetres) in length, and shaped like a straight sword with two cutting edges. They are made from ironwood. The handle is carved to give a good grip, generally being held by both hands.

Cooper's confidence and fighting skill was great and he managed to evade the Aborigine's attacks until he found his opportunity to bring home a tremendous smash on the skull of his opponent. The fight was over. Though the native was not killed, he was knocked unconscious, and the white man was proclaimed victor.

The following day was set aside for the next trial by battle, but the second challenger had lost heart and confidence, and in the first round of the spear-throwing received a wound in his left thigh which put him out of action. King Joe had established himself in the only fashion understood by his subjects. Cooper married a full-blooded native of Melville Island, who proved herself to be an excellent wife and devoted mother. She presented him with a son and two daughters.

There was hardly a dialect between Darwin and the Gulf of Carpentaria with which Robert Joel Cooper was unfamiliar. In buffalo-shooting he outclassed even America's famed Buffalo Bill. Altogether, he accounted for 27,000 buffaloes during his reign. In the museum at Adelaide there is a rifle with which he shot 3,000 of them.

King Joe was extremely fond of his son, Reuben. Like his great father, Reuben was tall and well-built, and a wonderful athlete. He was educated at Prince Alfred College, South Australia. Just before World War I the noted Australian athlete, Snowy Baker, chose Reuben, with some other young, outstanding sportsmen, to tour the world giving exhibitions of physical culture. Cooper senior was justly proud of this, and when the war caused the abandonment of the project he was a very disappointed man.

Before his death, the white ruler was acknowledged by all the people of the north as a man who had done more good for the former fierce Melville Island natives than anybody else who ever entered the Territory. His descendants today have proved themselves worthy children of a notable sire.

QUONG TART

Old Sydneyites often recall that remarkable personality Quong Tart, one of the leading merchants of Sydney in the latter part of the last century.

Though born in China of Chinese parents he became a thorough Australian and even collaborated with the great Australians of his day in art, literature, and politics.

He was a leading light in the Highland Society, of which he was a member, and was an authority on Scottish legend and history. It was his frequent whim to don the kilt, and he loved to call himself

MacTart. He spoke with an accent stronger than Harry Lauder's.

How did a Chinese become a member of a Highland Society? The explanation is simple.

In 1859 there came to Sydney a big batch of coolies. Among them a boy aged nine. Little Quong everybody on board called him. Although in the beginning he spoke only his native language, the lad learned a lot from the engineers on the voyage. (In those days, if you called down the ventilator of a steamer's engine-room: 'Are you there Mac?' one or more voices in broad Scots would invariably reply, 'Aye'.) Because of this, Quong's English had a Scottish flavour long before it could develop an Australian twang.

The gang of coolies to which the youngster belonged was sent to the district of Braidwood, New South Wales, to work on alluvial mines at Bell's Creek, owned by a prominent Scot. It was natural that this gentleman should be intrigued by the small Chinese boy who had picked up a few Scottish phrases. Soon Quong Tart was one of the household.

The boy acquired fluent English and acted as interpreter between his patron and the coolies who worked the mines. When it is said his English was fluent, it should be added 'as spoken in the land of the heather'.

Apart from the household of which Quong Tart was now a member, Braidwood was a community of Scots. So it was that from his early formative years this Chinese boy was turned into a Scotsman by his environment. That is why, when he returned to Australia after a visit to China, he greeted newspaper reporters with the remark: 'Ma foot is on ma native heath, ma name is now MacTart'.

There is no need to trace all the steps which led to Quong's accumulation of a great fortune. When he was only twenty-three years old, just fourteen years after he arrived in Braidwood as a penniless little coolie, the *Sydney Morning Herald* remarked that Mr Tart enjoyed such amazing popularity in Braidwood that the people were asking him to represent them in Parliament.

Eventually Quong Tart left Braidwood for Sydney. Here is a clipping from the *Sydney Morning Herald:* 'All classes and creeds united in entertaining him at a farewell banquet. Judge McFarland took the chair. The gathering included the leading men of the district.' (There is no need to list their names—most of them were Macs.) The account continues: 'The distinguished guest was eulogised and toasted, and presented with illuminated addresses, together with valuable presents in silver and gold. Mr Tart replied in manly and felicitous terms and sang *Auld Lang Syne.*'

And so to Sydney, to set up as a tea merchant. On to more success and fortune. He pioneered the modern restaurant. In that day Sydney could not boast of even one cafe where the citizenry could get light refreshments. A meal, yes, and a good meal for sixpence, even fourpence, but a bit rough, needless to say. It took a Chinese, now an educated, wealthy Chinese, to show Australia what a modern restaurant could be.

Quong Tart began with a series of cafes in Pitt and King Streets 'on a scale of splendour never seen in Australia'. In these cafes one could have a cup of tea or a full meal. This type of establishment is familiar and commonplace today. In the 1870s and 1880s it took Sydney by storm; and Quong Tart increased his wealth.

But money-making was not his main preoccupation. His philan-thropy was unlimited. Quong Tart made fortunes and gave back to

Australia all he won. In the Braidwood district, residents would show with pride a church he had given them, a schoolhouse, sportsground. In Sydney could be pointed out, in many directions, the gifts he had bestowed on the community. Apart from these benefactions, dozens of men admitted they owed their start in life to this generous Chinese. His fame spread throughout Australia.

A friend of mine is the proud owner of a collection of photographs of Quong Tart—as a Chinese Mandarin, as an officer in the uniform of the Australian military forces, and in the kilt, with bagpipes.

AMAZON OF THE MANNING RIVER

An extraordinary character in Australia's past was a woman named Isabella Mary Kelly who, in the middle of last century, ruled the Manning River district of New South Wales with a rod of iron. Few records of her remain, but it is known she was a sadistic flogger of convicts and a ruthless killer of the Aborigines; even darker deeds have been hinted at.

Why Isabella Kelly chose to lose herself in the wilds of a newly-settled outpost will never be known. Along the Manning River old-timers told strange stories of this mysterious woman; legends handed down the years—probably embroidered in the process—but, in the main, undoubtedly true and all of them grim.

One day, in the late 1830s, she came into the little township of Dungog and made straight to the office of the police magistrate, Captain Thomas Cook. Without a word of greeting she strode up to the magistrate, who was showing his new assistant his duties, and immediately began to state her business:

'I haven't time to waste, Captain. I've come all the way in from Brimbin especially to see you.'

'Pardon me a moment, Miss Kelly,' the magistrate replied, 'I'm showing my new assistant some important work'.

'You have all day and every day to attend to your "important" work! New assistant or old assistant I won't be put off! Now listen to me—'

The assistant asked to be excused to leave the room, but Isabella exclaimed:

'You can stay! This is no tete-a-tete! It matters not who is present when I have anything to say! My business is this, Captain. The blacks are proving troublesome. Some of my cattle at Brimbin are missing— no doubt the blacks have stolen them. I want you to send out an armed expedition to wipe out every native in the district.'

'Miss Kelly,' answered the magistrate, 'your request is too ruthless to consider! Moreover, I object to your overbearing manner. You seem to forget that I—'

'I forget nothing! Don't go beating about the bush! I want no humbugging in the matter. I demand that you send an expedition!'

'And I refuse!'

'Very well. I shall take matters into my own hands in the same way that I'm forced to do everything else. But I'm capable! I run my properties single-handed. I even save your public scourger here the job of punishing my convict servants by flogging them myself.'

'Undoubtedly you do a more thorough job than the public scourger. Your stark brutality to your convicts is known through out the countryside!'

'I treat my convict scum as they deserve to be treated! I know how to conduct my own affairs! And I know how to act now that you've refused my request. There won't be a black left alive within miles of my properties! I'll exterminate them myself!'

'That won't be surprising! Already you have a grim reputation as a killer of the blacks. Nor does it stop at blacks.'

'So you're referring to the settler who tried to squat on some of my land? If I waited for you fools of magistrates to act, nothing would be done! I am the law on my own property! Lucky for the wretched knave that I merely wounded him! Let it be a warning! If any trespasser dares to squat on my land again I'll put a bullet through his head!'

'Please leave my office, Miss Kelly! Your insolence is insufferable. I intend sending a full report to the Colonial Secretary informing him of your barbarous conduct to blacks and whites alike!'

'Do your damnedest, you incompetent nincompoop! What care I about your reports to the Colonial Secretary? You're an idiot—unfit to hold the post of magistrate!

'I came here with a request for those cursed blacks to be taught a lesson, though I might have known that I would be wasting my time with you! But by heavens I know how to use a gun, and I'll see to it that my district is free of the wretches for all time!'

As Miss Kelly strode out of the room, slamming the door, the assistant exclaimed:

'A veritable virago, if ever there was one! Who is that amazing woman?'

'You won't be long here before you'll learn all about her,' replied the magistrate. 'She's the uncrowned ruler of the Manning River district.'

'What authority has she?'

'None but her own. It's her stinging tongue, arrogance and vile temper that everyone fears—myself included. But make no mistake about it, her demeanour is not a mere bluff. She knows no mercy. She's womanhood's cruellest creature. She'll kill those natives in cold blood!'

'From where did this amazon come? Apparently she's been well-educated. What's her history?'

'There's not much known about her history. According to reports she was engaged to be married to an army officer in Dublin. It was to be a big social wedding and elaborate preparations were made for it, but on the wedding-day the bridegroom failed to arrive at the church. It's said that her jilted romance so embittered her that she fled from her friends and surroundings and came to this outlandish place.'

'When did she arrive here?'

'Some twenty years ago—nobody knows for certain. It seems that she was in her middle twenties, and she came with some thirty assigned convict servants.'

'Then apparently she was given her district as a land grant?'

'It's all very vague. Nobody knows about her private affairs or legal rights. She certainly lays claim to a tremendous slice of territory. She's divided it up into two huge station properties for cattle and horses.'

'And she runs both properties single handed?'

'Yes. She makes her convict servants work like slaves. The law states that when convicts need punishment they must be dealt with by the public scourger. But Isabella Kelly defies authority. She flogs the convicts herself. Her treatment of them is shocking. To give you an instance of her lack of all human decency: on one occasion she decided to take two of her convicts to Port Macquarie and have them put in the solitary confinement cells in the penal settlement there. Saddling up her horse, and with her pistols round her belt, she marched them off. On the way they were crossing a flooded river when her horse was swept from under her and she was thrown into the swiftly-flowing waters. One of the convicts, risking his own life, swam out after her and saved her from drowning. She showed her gratitude by forcing her saviour and his companion to continue marching to the penal settlement where she had them thrown into the dungeons!'

'What an inhuman monster! But surely you, as magistrate, have sufficient authority to put a stop to her diabolical actions?'

'The power of the magistrates is confined to the punishment of unruly convicts. We have little, if any, authority over their masters.'

'Then surely the Colonial Secretary will heed your report?'

'I've already sent him a report on Isabella Kelly, but nothing has been done in the matter. I can do no more than send in a further report about her. In the meantime, I'm afraid, she'll make short shrift of the natives.'

Sure enough, Isabella Kelly returned to Brimbin and, arming herself with gun and pistol, slaughtered the small Aborigine population camped there.

Again, nothing was done by the Chief Secretary and this infamous woman continued her reign of terror.

One day, towards the end of 1840, she set off from Brimbin with a consignment of hides and tallow to be sold at Maitland. Two convicts were in charge of the load and she accompanied them on horseback.

On the return trip, as they were crossing the range at Wallarobba, they were bailed up by a gang of bushrangers led by Edward Davis—known as the jewboy. The gang didn't bother the two convicts, but they tied Isabella to a wheel of the dray, took a pistol from her, and stole the £60 she had been paid for the hides and tallow.

When the gang left, Isabella ordered the convicts to set her free. She had another pistol concealed in her saddle-bag, and she set off after the bushrangers. She caught up with them after a 5-mile (8 kilometre) chase and opened fire, one bullet striking a bushranger in the shoulder. Not only did she make them return her money but other money they had in their possession. Eventually the members of this gang were rounded up by the troopers and hanged in Sydney.

By the 1860s Isabella Kelly was a wealthy woman. Brimbin and Mount George Stations in the Taree district had greatly prospered. Brimbin was located at the head of the Dawson River on the northern side and was used for cattle and horses. But now there was considerable settlement on the Manning, and newcomers began to squat on portions of the big territory which Miss Kelly claimed was her land. Finding that she could not scare them away, and unwilling to risk the drastic personal action that succeeded in the past when settlers were few, she invoked the aid of law. That settled her.

The Government appointed a Select Committee to inquire into her title. It was then found that she had no proof that any land grants had been made to her. Furthermore, she had taken no steps to record her title to any of the land.

The reign of Isabella Kelly, the woman who had ruled and terrorised the district for nearly thirty years, was over. She moved to Sydney and soon afterwards sailed for England. However, she returned later to end her days in Sydney. She died in 1897, friendless, alone, and almost forgotten. It is said that she compiled her life story for publication, but the manuscript disappeared after her death. It would have been a valuable historic document of the pioneering days, but it is doubtful if Isabella Kelly would have recorded the whole of her life story—there were so many sinister episodes.

The Bad Old Alan of Moorebank

The township of Liverpool, New South Wales, had aspirations of becoming a great sea-port, like its namesake in England. It was the dream of Governor Lachlan Macquarie that the village he founded would become a metropolis, with a great export trade moving up and down George's River. In

days gone by schooners used to sail up the George's River to Liverpool, which had all the appearances of a seaport, complete with inns bearing nautical names. But though Liverpool's ambitions were worthy, they were not found to be seaworthy. Today the river has silted up and carries only row-boats.

On the banks of the river opposite Liverpool is Moorebank. In that district there once dwelt a bad old man—a mass-murderer who got away with it. The old fellow used to coax members of ships' crews to work for him on his farm.

'What about it, sailor? It's a grand life working on a farm. And, after all, you can always go back to the sea when you feel like it. What's more, son, you'll be able to save quite a tidy bit of money.'

The old chap never had any difficulty in persuading a sailor to work for him. In due course the employee would remind him of the matter of wages.

'Oh—your pay? Yes—yes, of course! Let me see—how many weeks' wages are due to you? I'll settle your account this very day. Indeed I will. And let me tell you how pleased I am with your work.'

Then he would lead the unsuspecting seaman to the edge of a projecting cliff near by, and would point to a big eucalyptus tree.

'I say, sailor, do you think there's a bees' nest in that tree?

My eyesight is not as good as it used to be. The wife reckons she sees lots of bees coming from it. You'll have to stand a bit nearer the edge…'

A hearty push from behind, and over the cliff would topple the former employee. At the foot of the cliff the old man's half-caste wife would be waiting with a tomahawk to finish off the victim.

It was a fool-proof system—almost. But the day came when a police spy was sent to work on the farm to investigate rumours. The farmer, becoming suspicious of the supposed sailor, shot him dead.

When the investigator failed to return, a sergeant and eight soldiers were sent to the scene. They ransacked the farm but failed to find the secret tunnel where the farmer and his wife had gone into hiding. They did find, however, the illicit still for making rum, which added further to the farmer's ill-gotten gains.

It was a pity that the troops were not teetotallers. A pity, too, that they should find the rum so excellent that they partook of it in most generous quantities. In addition to being good the rum was exceedingly potent, and ere long the military men were oblivious to everything.

Then from out of his hiding-place came the old man. He soaked the soldiers' uniforms thoroughly with rum and set fire to the surrounding scrub. It was a midsummer's day and a strong wind was blowing. All that was left of the party of troops were a few fire-arms, some brass buttons and bones. Then, to complete his distinguished career, the gentleman farmer killed his wife.

What became of him nobody knows. He and his dogs disappeared into the bush. His tracks were traced as far as the Woronora River, and some of his clothes were found on a rock in that vicinity. But of the man himself, or his dogs, nothing was seen. The good folks of Liverpool maintained (and little wonder) that he'd been carried off by Lucifer. Certainly he was a disciple of the devil, if ever there were one.

CHARLOTTE BADGER—BUCCANEER

Australia had a woman pirate. Many remarkable women have graced or disgraced the pages of our past but surely none so extraordinary as Charlotte Badger. She was born in the slums of London and began her adolescent career as a pickpocket. Quick, intelligent, and endowed with more than her share of good looks, she diligently practised her chosen profession. Before she was out of her teens she was recognised by fellow criminals as one of the best pickpockets in London. But with all her cleverness the Law eventually caught up with her and in the year 1806 she was convicted at the Old Bailey and sentenced to transportation to New South Wales for the term of her natural life.

On the voyage out to this country the light-fingered lady formed a lasting friendship with another convict woman, Sarah Barnes; a friendship which was to lead them to amazing adventure in the South Seas. It was Charlotte who was the brains of the partnership. Sarah was amiable and placid, without any of the audacity of her friend, but she was willing to follow Charlotte's every direction.

Even on the voyage Charlotte confided to Sarah that she had no intention of ending her days in the convict settlement at Botany Bay and that she would plan an escape for them both.

The colony was only eighteen years old when they arrived and one can well imagine what a depressing place it was to Charlotte after the gaiety of London. More than ever she determined that the permanence of living death was not for her. Dimly at first, but with steadily growing clarity, she began to make her plans.

Some weeks later the colonial brig *Venus* was loading in Sydney Cove for Hobart Town. Superintending its loading was its hardworking, highly-respected mate, John Kelly. Little did Kelly think when he saw Charlotte Badger and Sarah Barnes come aboard with a gang of male convicts that these two women held in their hands his destiny, and that because of them he was to swing high from a gallows' tree a few years later. The two women had been assigned as convict servants in Hobart Town, hence their presence on the boat.

The moment Charlotte saw John Kelly she marked him as the key which was to open freedom for her and Sarah.

The *Venus* sailed and, two days after clearing Sydney Heads dropped anchor in Twofold Bay. The ship's boat carrying the captain swung away to the shore and Kelly was left in charge of the vessel—and in the hands of the temptress. Charlotte had not been wasting her time. Already she was able to influence Kelly to open a keg of rum and make merry with a foursome comprising herself, Sarah, the mate and a member of the crew.

In the midst of the revelry the captain returned. Infuriated, he had them flogged and put in irons, Kelly included. Nevertheless, Charlotte knew that her plan was working as she intended.

The *Venus* continued her voyage. As the brig rounded Cape Howe for the long run down the south-eastern coast, the captain realised that he needed the mate to help with the navigation. Grudgingly, he released Kelly but made the tactless error of telling him bluntly that on arrival in Hobart Town he intended having him arrested for neglect of duties.

Charlotte saw this as the logical fulfilment of events. She knew that John Kelly was ready for moulding into her momentous plans. She contrived to embitter him against authority, telling him that he would be convicted and sent to the hell of Port Arthur. On the other hand, there was always a south-sea island paradise where they could live happily—if they were free.

Whatever the blandishments Charlotte used, the mate secured all the firearms as the *Venus* neared Van Diemen's Land. He released three of the male convicts Charlotte picked as being suitable for her plans, and with Sarah and Charlotte gave them the guns.

Charlotte took immediate command. The crew was overpowered and with the rest of the convicts forced into the ship's boat and cut adrift. Before the captain entered the boat Charlotte flogged him on the deck of his own ship.

Then came the incredible career of Charlotte Badger, buccaneer. John Kelly remained the navigator, but Charlotte became the captain of the brig. At her command they intercepted another vessel on the high seas, raided it, and removed all food and firearms to their own ship. Then the mutineers sailed for New Zealand. Two trouser-clad women alternated their turns at watch on deck while four men struggled to sail the brig across the stormy Tasman Sea.

At last they reached the Bay of Islands, where they made friends with a Maori tribe. They off-landed their stores, scuttled the *Venus*, and settled down to peace among the reed and flax huts of the natives. In time Sarah migrated inland to Rotorua where she spent the rest of her life as the white wife of a Maori chieftain. Two of the convicts travelled with her and also married into the tribe.

Charlotte, however, remained at the Bay of Islands with Kelly and the other convict, despite the continual danger of a calling warship or a whaler. For eight years the mutineers lived unmolested until one day a man-o'-war sailed into the bay. The natives were bribed into handing over the two white men who were taken to England and hanged. Charlotte was not to be found. By some means she had been warned and had taken to the bush.

Her life for the next twenty years is unknown. According to reports she was next seen in 1818. In that year the American whaling vessel *Lafayette*, bound from San Franscisco to Newcastle, called at the island of Vavau in the Tongan Group. While getting fresh water supplies there the skipper was surprised to be addressed by a white woman. It was our fantastic friend, Charlotte Badger. She had a half-caste youth by her side—the child of herself and the native ruler of the island. She spoke Polynesian fluently and was quite candid with the Yankee skipper, telling him about her astonishing past. Apparently she was still an attractive personality for when the skipper sailed away from the island Charlotte accompanied him.

That is the last known of her. Where she went with her Yankee soulmate will never be discovered. Nor will anyone ever know whether she dragged him or subsequent lovers down to disaster as she did poor John Kelly.

The Eliza Emily Donnithorne Legend

In twelve secluded acres in Sydney, not far from the clatter of Newtown's shopping centre, is Camperdown Cemetery, one of Australia's most picturesque and historic burial grounds.

Beneath the crumbling headstones and grass-grown graves lie the remains of eighteen thousand Australian pioneers who struggled to build this nation in the lusty days of last century. As ever with death, the ancient cemetery knows no social discrimination. It rests the bones of Aborigines and aristocrats, the Emperor Napoleon's harpist, Nicholas

Charles Bochsa, and even of one man who claimed Royal blood. He was a former Commissioner of Police in New South Wales, and his headstone bears this inscription:

'Here lies the remains of William Augustus Miles, Police Magistrate and later Commissioner of Police, whose parentage was derived from Royalty. He was born in Hampshire, England, and died April 24th 1851 in the fifty-third year of his life, neglected and in poverty.'

A romantic tragedy surrounds the grave of Judge Donnithorne and his daughter Eliza Emily. The ornate headstone is inscribed:

In memory of

James Donnithorne

Esq.

For many years Governor of the Mint

and a judge in the Honourable East

India Company's Bengal Service.

Died 25th May 1852, aged 79 years.

Also of Eliza Emily

Last surviving daughter of the above.

Died 20th May 1886.

The poignant story of Eliza Emily Donnithorne and her lost love is one of old Newtown's most treasured legends. On a spring morning in the early 1850s there was much excitement and activity around a stately home on the corner of King Street and L'Avenue (now Georgina Street) in the then fashionable suburb of Newtown. The cream of Sydney society was thronging to the wedding of the wealthy Eliza whose fortune had been left to her by the late Judge Donnithorne. The beautiful bride-to-be had spared no expense for the celebrations which, after the nuptials, were to be held in an annexe in the grounds of the Donnithorne home. Crested carriages and sparkling broughams

converged at the entrance gates where the gentry emerged from the vehicles, the men in grey toppers, frock coats and canes, and their elegant ladies in crinolined gowns and holding frilled parasols in their long white-gloved hands. Gaiety was in the air as guests were introduced and entered the flower-decorated reception rooms, or strolled on the lawns waiting to escort the bridal couple to the nearby St Stephen's church. This somewhat unusual wedding procedure had been mentioned on the invitations.

Meanwhile the bridesmaids were putting the final touches to the arranging of Eliza's exquisite wedding gown. She looked radiant as she told them that everything looked perfect and they must not delay another moment before leaving for the church. But the bridesmaids had been informed that the groom had not arrived. Reluctantly they told her. Eliza was incredulous. What could have delayed him? Why had he sent no message? The bridesmaids comforted her, saying that he would surely arrive any moment. They fussed around her endeavouring to put her at her ease while they waited.

Time passed and still they waited. The guests' gaiety died down. Laughter turned to impatience and irritation, and then to embarrassment. There was nervous coughing as they speculated on the extraordinary situation. Was it possible, someone boldly suggested, that the groom had no intention of turning up? Gossip was whispered from group to group.

Another hour passed, and the dazed Eliza, still clutching her bridal bouquet, looked through her bedroom window to see guests mumbling their apologies and furtively departing.

Why the groom failed to appear has never been told, but the strange sequel to the story has been handed down the years. From the day she was jilted the heart-broken girl never left the house again, nor did she ever admit any visitors except her doctor and her solicitor. A housekeeper and another woman servant were her only communication with the outside world until her death thirty years later.

In all those long years, according to local legend, Eliza wore only her wedding garments, and the wedding cake on the banquet table was never disturbed as it gradually mouldered into dust and decay. Her eccentricity allowed no window to be opened, and every door was permanently locked, with the exception of the front door, which remained ajar on a chain. This, said the folks of old Newtown, was a sign that she expected her lover to come back some day.

The Donnithorne home no longer stands. A big business warehouse occupies the site in the no-longer fashionable area.

Unlike most legends, the story of Miss Donnithorne, or at least the essentials of the story, can be supported by factual evidence. A man who sold Bibles from house to house has left this written account of a visit to Miss Donnithorne's home:

'When I knocked on the door it was opened on the chain by an elderly attendant. Behind her I saw a person who must have been Miss Donnithorne. She was tall and stately and was clad all in white. The attendant took the book and both retired to a room off the entrance hall. Presently the maid returned with money and bought a Bible.'

In 1912 the sexton of St Stephen's Church, Mr R. Clark, told a Sydney newspaper reporter that he lived near the Donnithorne home as a child and had occasionally glimpsed her. He said that the front door was chained and that a big mastiff would lie just inside the door. 'There had been an unhappy romance, all right,' the sexton added.

After Mr Clark's statement appeared in the newspaper it was learned that the two attendants on Miss Donnithorne were still alive and had retired on an annuity left them by their eccentric mistress. A reporter traced their whereabouts and endeavoured to interview them. The encounter was a brief one. A very old lady opened the door to the newspaperman but refused to have anything to say. The reporter was persuasive and begged to be told some little thing about Miss Donnithorne. The ancient hesitated but suddenly a warning voice came from a room near the door: 'We know nothing—our lips are sealed in silence!' The door was then gently but firmly closed.

Though a self-imposed prisoner within the walls of her home, Miss Donnithorne was not unmindful of the poor and distressed in the outside world. Through her solicitor she did much to help the needy. 'Miss Donnithorne possessed a truly kind heart,' said one writer after her death. 'The great trouble which darkened her life and wrecked her hopes could not sour the natural sweetness of her disposition. She is still held in grateful remembrance at Newtown for her many acts of unobtrusive benevolence. Possessed of ample means, she gave freely to all comers and was never known to turn a deaf ear to the cry of distress.'

There is an extraordinary resemblance in the stories of Miss Donnithorne and Miss Havisham of Dickens' *Great Expectations*. Both women were jilted at the last moment and lived the remainder of their lives in seclusion wearing their bridal gowns and never permitting the festive wedding table to be touched.

It has been claimed that Miss Donnithorne was the original of Miss Havisham and that Dickens learned of the Newtown story and so received his inspiration. Those who refute the claim say that he would not have known of this story when he wrote *Great Expectations* as his sons only came to Australia later. However, Australian historian Mary M. Hegarty, in a lecture before members of the Australian Catholic Historical Society on 'Charles Dickens and Australia', put forth strong evidence in support of the supposition that Miss Donnithorne was indeed the original Miss Havisham.

On 30th March 1850, Dickens brought out the first issue of a weekly periodical, *Household Words*, which flourished for ten years and in its day became the most widely-read periodical in England. From the very first issue Australia was widely publicised as a land of opportunity. Australian stories and sketches appear steadily through the issues. 'Pictures of Life in Australia,' 'A Bundle of Emigrants' Letters,' 'Two-handed Dick the Stockman,' 'John Chinaman in Australia'. The latter article, which appeared in the issue of 17th April 1858, is a most detailed colourful word-picture of the Chinese people who were at that time a numerous section of the Australian population. The exactness of the observations indicates that the writer was undoubtedly an eye-witness. There are articles on gold-diggers, a Digger's Diary, and even the story of Fisher's Ghost is told with much emphasis on the eeriness of the tale. Wainewright, the elegant painter-poisoner convict, Sir Henry Brown Hayes and the Irish sods he placed around his Vaucluse home to drive the snakes away—all these stories Dickens included in his *Household Words*.

Great Expectations was published in 1860–61, and Dickens had then been receiving and printing stories of Australian life for ten years. Miss

Donnithorne was still alive in 1860 (she lived to 1886) so that naturally her story was disguised as fiction.

THE EULO QUEEN

Of all the stories which still are told around the camp fires of south-west Queensland none is more colourful than that of the Eulo Queen, for this ravishing beauty, amazing horsewoman, and unscrupulous siren was the Australian counterpart of the 'Diamond Lils' and 'Klondyke Kates' of American frontier mining camps.

Eulo, about forty miles west of Cunnamulla, in the far south-west corner of Queensland, is today a ghost town whose only callers are drovers making the long trek down the Paroo country with mobs of travelling stock. A fire many years ago destroyed the old Eulo Hotel where the Queen held court. Her real name is not known for certain although some old-timers claim that it was Isobel Gray. It was enough that she was the Queen, the Eulo Queen, the toast of squatters from Charleville to Bourke. These gentry drank their toasts in nothing but champagne, which the young hostess brought to her back-of-beyond hotel by dray and packhorse 700 miles (1100 kilometres) from Brisbane.

In the early 1890s Eulo was a wild, rip-roaring little town with several hotels serving the needs of the army of opal miners in the nearby Duck Creek and other fields. In this womanless west the beauty and seductive personality of the Eulo Queen were legendary. Stockmen, shearers and drovers 'knocked down' their pay cheques at her pub, rarely leaving until they had spent their last pound. Miners showered her with gems; she was reputed to have the finest collection of opals in the world.

The Eulo Queen is immortalised in much of Queensland's early fiction and poetry. Steele Rudd introduced her into several of his short stories, and Barcroft Boake makes reference to her in the ballad 'Skeeta', when he tells of the selector's daughter waiting by the sliprails for her drover lover to return from Queensland and how she learns that he had been seen drinking and riding with the Eulo Queen.

Eventually the Queen's scandalous conduct became too much even for the tough little township of Eulo, and the police, forced to take action, debarred her from holding a hotel licence. She easily surmounted this difficulty by getting one of her many men friends to 'dummy' for her as the licensee, and another to take her on a world tour until things quietened down. Her travelling companion was a wealthy squatter but he returned penniless from the trip, even though the Queen was ablaze with diamonds.

She settled into her old life, but now she found that Eulo was on the decline. The opal fields were petering out and the population dwindling. She determined, however, that come what may she would never forsake her 'domain'. The passing of the years took heavy toll of her beauty and her wealth, and she was one of the last remaining residents of Eulo when she died in 1925 in her nineties.

CHRISTY PALMERSTON

In the 1880s Christy Palmerston was a legendary name to the people of Northern Queensland. A man of mystery, little was known of his early life, but it was claimed that he was the natural son of Lord Palmerston, Prime Minister of Great Britain, and Countess Carandini, a famous Italian opera singer and beauty.

What brought Christy Palmerston to Australia is a matter of conjecture, but soon after his arrival he accompanied the James Venture Mulligan expedition to the Upper Mitchell River in 1874. Despite his excellent education he was a somewhat shady character whose dealings were not always within the Law, yet he was a true pioneer who did much to open up the wild, unknown country of the north.

Palmerston was a mild-mannered little man with a withered arm. He rejected civilisation and chose the company of Aborigines. No one knew where he lived and whenever he made his brief visits to the townships he wore an overcoat, cabbage tree hat and dark glasses, and was always attended by a bodyguard of Aboriginal warriors.

His misdeeds included the robbing of the Chinese who thronged the North Queensland goldfields. The Chinese were terrified of the strange little man and his black bodyguard and always fled at his approach, leaving gold behind them which the white man promptly pocketed. A tale is told that on one occasion they laid a trap for him that nearly cost him his life. When they fled as before, Palmerston picked up one of the usual little chamois bags in which the Chinese kept their gold, and untied the draw-string. His quick eye caused him to jerk his hand away a split second before the fangs of a death-adder struck forth.

It wasn't only the Chinese whom Palmerston robbed. He is known to have cheated white settlers by showing them samples of gold and promising to tell them where he had found the specimens on payment of a lump sum. In this way he received several hundred pounds at various times, but there was never any gold discovered at the sites he indicated.

Christy Palmerston was responsible for subduing some of the wildest jungle natives in the Cape York Peninsula. When word reached him of the deaths of three white men speared by a tribe of these natives he set off on the trail of the murderers with a rifle and his bodyguard and dealt out his own mode of justice. It was a savage form of retribution, judging by the many bullet-riddled skulls afterwards found at the site of the murders.

This remarkable little man never carried camping gear and learned to live like the natives, eating whatever the bush afforded, often the roots of plants, grubs and snakes. His trail-blazing through thick jungle between the scattered white settlements opened up much territory hitherto regarded as inaccessible. He was the first white man to explore the Mulgrave, the Herbert, the Beatrice, the Tully, the North and South Johnstone, the Russell, and the Barron Rivers at their headwaters. He discovered the Daintree Pass and opened the way to Port Douglas. Today the name of this legendary mystery man is remembered on the north Queensland map in the East Palmerston and West Palmerston areas and the Palmerston Highway.

Dr Robinson

In the early 1860s there was no one more popular in the Lachlan River district of New South Wales than Dr Robinson. He was a handsome man over 6 feet (180 centimetres) tall and proportionately built. He wore a long cutaway coat with a waistcoat buttoned up to the throat. The waistcoat was single-breasted and carried a row of bright steel buttons so that at a distance he could have been mistaken for a trooper, especially as he invariably wore riding breeches and high Wellington boots. This costume more than once nearly cost him his life.*

About ten o'clock one night in 1863 Dr Robinson was ready to turn in. He had had a strenuous day and had not long returned from attending a patient 10 miles (16 kilometres) from the town of Forbes, where he resided. He was congratulating himself that he would have a good night's rest, when there came a loud knocking at his front door, followed by a vigorous pull on the bell.

'Just my luck,' he muttered, 'Another false alarm of that Mrs Noonan. The woman is a confounded nuisance.'

'Hello!' he exclaimed as he recognised Jim Stubbs, a stockrider from Hopover sheep station. 'What's the matter, Jim?'

'Well, sir,' said the man, touching his hat, 'there's been a bit of an accident. Jack Banks has gone and shot himself.'

Bidding the man enter the doctor asked, 'What made him do that? Drinking?'

'Oh, no, sir, he didn't mean to shoot himself on purpose. He and a couple of shearers were out kangaroo shooting and well I don't know exactly how it happened, sir.'

'Whereabouts is he shot?'

'Somewhere about here, sir,' replied Jim, passing his hand indefinitely inside the left thigh and over the groin. 'The boss packed me off for you, sir.'

The doctor was puzzled.

'I can't understand how any man could shoot himself with a gun in that part of the body. What time did the accident happen?'

'About three o'clock, sir,' was the reply.

'But Hopover station is no more than ten miles from here! And you never thought of coming for me till this time of night!' exclaimed the doctor.

'Well, sir, we didn't think it were very serious.'

'Indeed! Did the bullet make an exit?' the doctor enquired.

'Make a—beg pardon, sir?'

'Did it come out?' he demanded.

'No, sir,' the man answered.

* One such instance concerns this story which is still told in the district.

'Do you mean to tell me that your boss, Mr Riddleton, thought that a bullet in a man's groin was not a serious matter, and that he postponed sending for me till this time of night?' The doctor's tone was wrathful.

'I—er—don't think as how the boss had been a-rightly told as to the—er—,' faltered the man uncomfortably.

'Righto, righto! I'll get my horse saddled. Here, help yourself to a drop of Scotch in the meantime.'

After saddling his horse Dr Robinson returned to the room and put a small case of surgical instruments into one of his capacious pockets. At the same time he put a revolver in an inner breast pocket. Leaving the house with his caller they mounted their horses and set off at a brisk trot.

For a mile or so the doctor was in the lead. So rapid was his pace that his companion had to canter his horse to keep up with him. Soon, however, the country became rougher and the pace had to be reduced. Great masses of black clouds came rolling up from the south-east and obscured what little light the moon gave forth. Big raindrops, scouts of the coming storm, began to fall and very soon were succeeded by torrents of rain. None but a man like the doctor or his companion could have travelled on such a night in the black shadows of the bush at much beyond a walking pace. Like sailors accustomed to peer far into the night across the dark seas for the faint glimmer of a tiny light they could distinguish objects that would have been invisible to a city-bred man. Moreover, their horses, left practically to their own instincts, avoided every obstacle.

They had covered about 8 miles (13 kilometres)—the storm had passed to the north—when they came to a spot where the road forked. The doctor rode on straight ahead, but Jim Stubbs halted and called after him, 'This road, doctor!'

The doctor pulled up and shouted back, 'This is the road to the station!'

'That's so,' replied Stubbs, 'but he—he's not at the station.' Dr Robinson walked his horse back to where the road branched off. His anger was apparent from his tone.

'You told me the man was at Hopover station! Why didn't you speak the truth? Where is this wounded man?'

'He's at the Billy Can pub, sir. If I'd told you he wasn't at the station mebbe you wouldn't a come,' replied Stubbs.

'The Billy Can is more than 5 miles [8 kilometres] from here—and a wretched road, too,' exclaimed the doctor. 'It would serve you right if I turned back.'

'Don't do that, doctor! You'll be paid well, sir.'

'Confound you, I wasn't thinking of the payment,' replied the doctor angrily, as he took the new road.

The Billy Can Hotel was a bush shanty where the coach changed horses twice a week. The proprietor, 'Ratty' Bob Mason, had a poor reputation and was strongly suspected by the police of being in league with the outlaws who scoured the bush.

Dr Robinson, however, was a fearless man and could use the little weapon he carried in his breast pocket with deadly effect if called upon to act on the defensive. He also reasoned that his services were evidently required by whom he knew not—and that, therefore, he would be unmolested.

He pushed ahead regardless of the broken nature of the country till he came to the brow of a steep hill at the foot of which the lights of the Billy Can twinkled.

He was a good 40 yards (36 metres) in front of Stubbs when a man stepped out of the bush and pointed the barrel of a gun at him.

He pulled up his horse and quickly put his hand into his breast pocket, when Stubbs rushed up and shouted, 'It's the doctor!' Instantly the threatening weapon was lowered.

The doctor smiled. He began to see reason for his midnight visit.

'Blimey!' said the stranger to Stubbs as he drew up, 'I took him for a trooper!' Jim Stubbs nodded and rode on with the doctor.

Arriving at the Billy Can, they rode into the small stockade at one end of which were some stables and outbuildings. Giving his horse to Stubbs, who promised to rub him down and look after him, the doctor walked toward the main entrance. He noticed three or four rough-looking men at different parts of the premises, each carrying a gun. 'The kangaroo shooters,' said the doctor to himself with a wry smile, 'seem unwilling to relinquish their weapons.'

Here a man stepped out and said, 'Your patient is in here, sir,' indicating a small room used for stowing away old harness, lumber, and odds and ends. There, on a stretcher lay a brown bearded man of about thirty years of age.

'You've been long enough coming, doctor,' said this man.

'Thirteen miles [21 kilometres] on a night like this, and over such country in an hour and ten minutes is not such bad time,' replied the doctor looking at his watch.

'Hold the lantern here and let me see the wound,' he said to the man who had directed him to the room. The patient was stripped of his riding breeches. Dr Robinson opened his instrument case and then began probing for the bullet. He found that it had struck the inside of the thigh, having evidently been deflected, missing the bone and vital arteries in a miraculous manner, and had lodged just beneath the skin at the back of the thigh. Turning the patient over, he made a couple of incisions and presently drew out the leaden messenger.

A single glance told him at once that the bullet had come from a police carbine. There was also a slight dent in it. 'You've had a narrow escape. How did you manage to shoot yourself?' queried the doctor with a grin.

The patient was indignant at the question.

'Who said I shot myself? D'ye think I'm a flamin' kid?'

'The bullet must have struck something before entering your body, to take the direction it did,' explained the doctor.

'Yes—it hit a buckle on the saddle,' he was told.

'Then you can thank the buckle for probably saving your life,' said the doctor tersely.

'Give me the bullet, doctor.' This was done, and the man took his pocket-knife and cut a notch in the head.

Meantime, the doctor plugged up the hole, stitched, and did all that was necessary to make the patient comfortable.

'The wound is not so serious, as it happens; you'll be able to get about in a few days. Meantime, you had better have a good rest, otherwise inflammation may set in.'

A great laugh from the patient greeted this advice. 'Rest! A few days! Me! Not much! I rode 40 miles [65 kilometres] with that bullet in me. Blast me, if I can't ride twice that distance now it's out!' Here he held up the piece of lead between his forefinger and thumb. 'See here, doctor—I'll send this bullet back to him that sent it! You'll know it again! But the next time you look for it you'll pick it out of a trooper's skull!'

The doctor left the room and went to see how his horse fared. One of the men was leaning over the stable door looking at it. 'That's a bit of good horseflesh, sir. Will you part with him?'

'He's not for sale,' answered the doctor curtly as he left and re-entered the house.

Satisfied with a glass of the Billy Can's best whisky and a biscuit, Dr Robinson flung himself upon a sofa, intending after an hour's rest to make a start for home. Instead, he fell into a sound slumber, and it was daybreak when he awoke. The landlord had thrown a rug over him. He rose hastily and his first thought was for his horse. He hurried to the stable and was greeted with a whinnied note as the horse left off feeding. Jim Stubbs had looked after him.

The strange men and their horses were nowhere to be seen. The patient, too, was gone. An enquiry from the landlord elicited the information that they had all left hours ago.

'But,' added Ratty Bob, 'you'll be paid all right, doctor.'

The latter gave a look of contempt and prepared to return to Forbes.

A month later the doctor received by post a bank draft for fifty guineas, accompanied by a handsome gold watch on which were engraved his own initials, with the date of his attendance on his unknown patient. The watch was brand new and had been purchased in Forbes. He kept it, but having suspicions about the bank draft he distributed the money to charity.

Six months later Dr Robinson decided to move to Wagga Wagga. As there were no railways in that part of New South Wales all his goods had to be taken on a bullock wagon.

The doctor, sitting alongside the driver of his baggage, had got about half-way on the journey, and was in rough country, when a man rode out of the bush and, putting a gun to his shoulder, called out, 'Put your hands up! And don't—oh, it's you, Dr Robinson! My humble apologies!'

With a smile the armed man spurred his horse and disappeared into the bush.

WAGGA WAGGA IN THE 1880S

'Can you beat that! Were we lucky! Did you see who that was?' exclaimed the driver.

'Yes—I remember him now. He was a patient of mine at the Billy Can,' the doctor replied.

'I dunno about him being a patient, but I do know that that was bushranger Ben Hall.'

The worthy doctor never had to perform the unpleasant task of picking the bullet from the skull of a trooper, for Ben Hall was himself riddled by more than thirty bullets when he was ambushed shortly afterward.

Dr Robinson remained at Wagga Wagga, where he was revered by the pioneers of those early days, until he died some years later.

Rockhampton and the Magpie

In 1854, Colonel O'Connell, Government Resident of the district of Gladstone, received a memo from the Governor of Queensland, Sir Charles Fitzroy, thanking him for sending him samples of gold picked up in the district. Although the Government Resident had stated that the samples were probably isolated pieces and that there appeared to be no other gold in the vicinity, His Excellency considered it an encouraging sign and begged that no effort be spared in trying to locate a profitable field. Such a find, he added, would bring prosperity to the country and be a valuable aid to colonisation.

Acting on the Governor's wishes Colonel O'Connell did all in his power to locate the elusive metal. It was not until four years later that there was any definite result. A Cornish miner named Chapple, known as 'The Magpie' because of his voluble tongue, had been commissioned to explore the Fitzroy River country. He returned to Gladstone with the news that he'd found what he was after at Canoona.

The none too-prosperous townsfolk were crowded round the Government Resident's office when 'The Magpie' emerged to tell them the glad tidings.

'Look at it, folks!' he cried. 'Parcels of rich alluvial gold! And all of it gleaned from just simple dish-washing! It's there in bucketfuls! California has nothing on Canoona! And if it's in Canoona it must be elsewhere! I've been a miner all my life. I've been a prospector on the

Klondyke—in California—El Dorado—all over the world—and be-lieve me I know gold country when I see it. And this is it—sure! There's gold for everyone, so help me. I'm promising you this that we'll all be—' His voice was lost in the cheering as the crowd surrounded him and escorted the hero down to the pub to celebrate.

Fired by 'The Magpie's' golden tongue the people of Gladstone began their great exodus. Soon the little town was all but deserted; even the publican quitted. In letters to the south news of the discovery went forth. From southern Queensland they came, abandoning farms, stations and villages. Hot upon their heels came shiploads of prospec-tors pouring into Gladstone.

It was found that Gladstone was not the most advantageous point of disembarkation, but the Fitzroy River close by the goldfields proved navigable for some miles inland. A tiny business community sprang up where the vessels discharged their cargo. Thus were laid the founda-tions of Rockhampton.

But what of the gold? 15,000 men, with the number ever growing, were now on the field but only a few were getting any results. Murmurs of discontent arose among the frustrated majority; they were sullen and disillusioned. Food supplies were running low, and the corresponding high prices demanded incensed the prospectors, most of them without any resources. Faced with starvation they gave way to violence. They looked for a scapegoat—Chapple—'The Magpie'.

A mob of angry diggers were voicing their grievances at an open-air meeting when a group approached holding Chapple as a prisoner.

'We found him at the Bush Inn, where he always is—drinking his grog and talking—talking—talking!' shouted the leader of the group. 'Well,' he added, 'he won't be able to talk his way out of this! Tie the rope round his neck and string him up on the tree! The Magpie's made his last croak!'

The crowd's attention was suddenly diverted at the sight of Commissioner Cloote forcing his way through their midst as he cried out, 'Order! Order! In the name of Her Majesty's Government! What's the meaning of this? Mob rule! Lynching! I demand that you observe the law of the land!'

A digger stepped forward and faced the Commissioner when he reached the centre of the meeting. 'You're a brave man. Commissioner Cloote, but this is the law of the people! That man lured us from our homes with the promise of gold, and left us to starve. The traitor falsely claimed there was gold for everybody. He's a braggart—an imposter! But now he'll pay the penalty—'

'Hold on,' interrupted Cloote. 'Surely you're blaming Chapple too harshly for all the troubles here. Maybe out of vanity he exaggerated the importance of his discovery. But remember this. When he promised gold for everyone he didn't foresee the multitude that was to flock to the field. When Chapple made his rash declaration he was talking to the people of Gladstone. And in that regard he was probably right. After all, gold has been found here.'

'Commissioner Cloote,' replied the digger, 'I'm a Gladstone man, and I was present when "The Magpie" said there was gold to be found not only in Canoona but all round it! For that lie, alone, he deserves to be strung up!'

Amid the shouts of approval the Commissioner made a desperate decision. 'Have you tested Chapple's claim yourself?' he asked. 'Have you proved it false? Let's experiment. Some of you men have picks and shovels ,with you. Why not do a little digging here where we stand and see what the earth yields. The unwritten law of the digger is to give every man a fair go!'

At Commissioner Cloote's suggestion the men dug. The miracle happened. When the first pan of dirt was washed it gave nearly a half-ounce of gold. In the mad scramble that followed, the mob's grievance against Chapple was completely forgotten. The ill-used prospector was left standing in the open, white-faced and dazed. He staggered away as if in a dream. Soon afterwards he vanished into the wilderness west of the Dawes Range—never to return.

Today Chapple is forgotten. Yet, despite his faults, he was a true pioneer and the fact remains that the city of Rockhampton is directly obliged to him for its birth.

The Man Who Saw a Unicorn

Ever since Captain Phillip planted his colony on the shores of Sydney Cove, Garden Island* has had more or less connection with the Navy. In the first fortnight of the settlement of New South Wales the island was allocated to the crew of HMS *Sirius* as a place where they might make a vegetable garden. Even today you may see on Garden Island carved upon a rock the date 1788 and two sets of initials belonging to members of the gardening party. Succeeding naval ships inherited the garden on the island so that they also might have a chance of enjoying a vegetable diet in port.

Of all the people who have lived on Garden Island since it was first occupied, the strangest tenant was Dr Brandt. We first hear of the doctor in the journal of Lieutenant Grant in command of the armed brig *Lady Nelson*. This naval vessel was on her voyage to New South Wales when she made the usual call at the Cape of Good Hope. Grant was in need of a person who combined medical knowledge with an interest in natural history, and when Dr Brandt was recommended to

* Now a dockyard of the Royal Australian Navy.

him he engaged him to be attached to the naval base in New South Wales.

He proved to be an eccentric German who had many extraordinary adventures to relate of his extensive wanderings in Africa. Indeed, he claimed the existence of the unicorn and asserted that he had seen one. Dr Brandt had two companions a dog and a baboon which, according to his stories, were the faithful and useful companions of his wanderings. Especially was he indebted to the baboon, which he said had saved him from starvation by digging up edible roots. Lieutenant Grant was obliged, therefore, to allow the dog and baboon to accompany the doctor on the vessel.

Dr Brandt suffered very much from sea-sickness on the voyage and vowed never to sail on another ship. Alas, his stay on Garden Island was not a happy one. The eccentric German was made a butt of the riff-raff of Sydney. The uncouth inhabitants used to make surreptitious visits to Garden Island to glimpse the big grey African baboon and his master who claimed to have seen a unicorn. Dr Brandt with the baboon and dog were the only inhabitants of the island when Lieutenant Grant and the *Lady Nelson* were absent from Port Jackson on service.

Many varieties of mankind have dwelt on Garden Island since the Navy first had dealings with it, but there have probably been none quite as remarkable as Dr Brandt and his two companions.

CAPTAIN PIPER

The first man in Sydney to bear the title of Comptroller of Customs was Captain Piper. He was a dashing Scotch officer, the only man in Sydney who drove a coach with four horses, and a typical specimen of the full-blooded sporting characters of those days. His famous dinners were much sought after. An old Scotch piper was always in attendance on the worthy captain, and a band discoursed national and spirited airs when the conviviality was on a large scale, which was very often.

Eventually the inevitable happened and he crashed financially. Sooner than become a shadow of his former glory, unhonoured and unsung, he determined to end his life on as grand a scale as he had lived. Manning a boat with some of his friends, together with a brass band, they rowed well down the harbour, through the Heads and out on to the rolling seas of the Pacific. After many rounds of grog, interspersed with songs and music, the captain shouted: 'Now then lads, "God Save the King".' The band struck up the anthem; the boat rocked and tossed on the billows; the gallant captain waved to his friends; then, with resignation in his soul, he commended his body to the fishes and plunged overboard.

Alas for his determination. A stalwart sailor leaned over and fastened a boat-hook to the captain's pants so that he just floundered ingloriously. They bundled the would-be suicide into the boat and landed him damp and shivering at Circular Quay.* Soon afterwards he went to Bathurst and settled on the land, where history records simply that he had many happy days. Today he is commemorated in the exclusive district called Point Piper.

GRANNY SMITH AND HER FAMOUS APPLE
Australia has done little to honour the memory of the woman who, from a stray tree that grew by chance, developed and marketed an entirely new variety of apple that is now universally acclaimed. It has been described as 'the world's most valuable apple—one with no faults and many virtues'.

The woman was Maria Ann Smith, better known as Granny Smith. Her only memorial is her tombstone alongside the church of St Anne's, Ryde, overlooking the Parramatta River. We are not yet a nation of venerators of the traditional.

The Granny Smith is unique among apples inasmuch that there is none its equal for cooking purposes, it is a splendid eating apple, and when stored keeps better than any other variety. Indeed, it has brought greater returns to Australian growers than all others combined.

Maria Smith came to Australia from England in the early 1800s. With her was her husband, Thomas, a daughter and two sons. (In all, Mrs Smith bore her husband sixteen children but nearly all died in childbirth.) They bought a few acres of land at what is now Eastwood, near Ryde, about 12 miles (20 kilometres) from Sydney. With a couple

---

*This story was told to me by the late Reverend Father Piper, OFM, a descendent of Captain Piper.

of cows, some fowls, and a few vegetables, the Smiths supported themselves by selling their produce while their fruit trees were growing to maturity.

Right from the beginning, Maria Ann seems to have been the chief breadwinner of the family. 'Upon her fell the whole of the responsibility until her sons Charles and William had grown. Her husband, Thomas Smith, took little part in the control of the orchard,' admits one of the very few records relating to her family.

In 1933, when there was some talk of erecting a memorial to Granny Smith, letters appeared in the press from old-timers who remembered her in their childhood or had heard their parents speak of her. One writer said, 'She walked to Ryde every Monday to catch the boat, returning home on Friday night. I can still picture her in her quaint poke bonnet, the apron that she always wore, and the old-fashioned, two-lidded basket she always carried.'

When their trees were grown, Granny Smith had taken a stall in the city markets, so becoming Sydney's (and possibly Australia's) first woman fruit agent. This hard-working housewife and business woman returned to the farm in the weekends, when she caught up with the housework, after her weekdays at the markets—for it was too far in those days for her to go home except on Friday night.

All her produce was packed in cases labelled 'From Granny Smith's Farm'. However, stories of how the first Granny Smith apple tree was grown are conflicting. Some maintain that it was merely a sport—a bud and branch which produced fruit different from that on the rest of the tree; or a seedling, whose fruit was different from the apple whose seeds were planted.

An account in the Tasmanian *Courter*, published in the 1890s, states: 'In 1867 the wife of Mr Thomas Smith…brought home some fruit cases from the Sydney markets. In the bottom of one case were the remains of some Tasmanian apples, known as French Crabs, and, the fruit being in a decayed condition, Mrs Smith emptied it on the bank of the creek which ran past her farm…' This seems to be the story generally accepted by horticultural writers.

The discovery that one of those rotting apples took root and grew up hidden among ferns and long grass is credited to a twelve-year-old boy, the son of a Mr E. H. Small. The boy, having tasted the fruit, told Mrs Smith what he had found and said that though the apples were green they tasted better than any he had ever eaten. (At that time only three varieties of apples were grown in Australia.)

Granny investigated the boy's discovery and as a result she propagated the new variety, applying to it all her wisdom and a lifetime of apple-lore. In due course the fruit was taken down to the markets by Granny—poke bonnet, apron, two-lidded basket and all—and there displayed in her cases marked 'From Granny Smith's'. From that the apple derived its name.

The new variety won immediate favour and brought higher prices than the others. Buyers who kept cases of the apples on hand were astonished at its keeping qualities and their reports testified to its virtues. Fellow orchardists were keen to grow the new apple and soon Granny was adding to her income by supplying young trees to others in the trade.

Granny Smith died in her seventieth year in 1870. The orchard was willed to her two sons Charles and William, but in time with the growth of Eastwood as a residential area it was sold, subdivided, and submerged beneath the tiled roofs of suburbia. Alas, the famous parent tree, which would have been of great importance to horticulturalists,* was chopped down, grubbed out, and burnt. Its millions of descendants—for the Granny Smith is now grown all over the world—are the living memorials of this indomitable pioneer.

*And surely of much interest to every Australian.

WHALING DAYS AND WAYS

The Whalers; A Whale of a Sea Story.

THE WHALERS

Man was a hunter for long years before he became a pastoralist and a breeder. Maybe the hunting instinct has left something still in his make-up, and that is why for well over a century stories of whaling on the high seas have had such appeal to the world's public. Today, of course, attitudes have changed; there being no neccessity to extract the oil, the world community have rightly joined to stop the practice. However, we can still enjoy the rollicking tales from the past when whaling was a necessary and thriving industry.

In their hunting quest the whaling men sailed into seas where white men had never been, charted islands, reefs and coastlines, fought with cannibals, suffered shipwreck, sudden death and slow torture. Oil for the lamps of the Old and the New World was what they sought, and in finding it they wrote some of the most exciting pages of Australia's story.

In 1804 the whaling industry was bringing to New South Wales alone £190,000 annually. American whalers made their first appearance in Australian waters in 1819 and between 1830 and 1850 they operated along the south-east and southern coasts in great numbers. Eyre's journal of 1845 gives the number of their ships for that year in Australian southern waters as three hundred.

Hobart in the 1840s was a lusty whaling town, second in size only to Sydney. It had over one hundred licensed drinking-houses, apart from the innumerable sly-grog shops that spring up around any port. Grog was cheap and plentiful, and indeed was the currency of the day. Crews from the men-o'-war fought with the whalers. In many a riot, where the tars put up a barrage by whirling open clasp-knives at the end of lanyards, the whalers used their harpoons.

The whaling crews provided a bright note even in that day of colourful uniforms, with their high-heeled boots, white corduroy trousers, loose white jerseys, topped with either a red or blue coat, indicating the watch to which the wearer belonged. A loose scarf around the throat and a low-crowned grey hat completed the uniform.

It is said that from their hats the captains knew when men were available for signing on. A whaler fresh from the sea, with a pocketful of money, turned his hat brim down as he set forth for a good time ashore. Eventually, when broke and unable to get further credit at the taverns, he flicked up the brim of his hat as a sign that he was ready to go to sea again.

The life was arduous and ill-paid, and wild crews sailed aboard the whalers. The Yankee captains chose men of all colours and creeds to lessen the chance of their combining to mutiny. Between the American and Australian crews great rivalry existed. A story is told of crews of both countries racing to be the first to harpoon a whale, when the American men executed a swift manoeuvre which brought their vessel between the whale and the Australian crew. 'That's how Americans do it!' shouted the Yankees. The skipper of the Australian whaler stood up in the bows and threw his harpoon clear over the American boat into the whale. 'And that's how we do it!' he shouted back.

To this period belongs one of the strangest, starkest tragedies of the sea. On 13th November 1819 the whaler *Essex* ran into a large school of whales off the coast of Tasmania. While the boats were out a huge whale rose to the surface and charged the ship, tearing away the keel. The monster then attacked a second time at full speed. As ship and whale met in a head-on collision the planking smashed like matchwood, and the ship heeled over.

Those of the crew who survived suffered incredible hardships before they were rescued, months later. One boat that was picked up contained two survivors of the original ten. When their provisions were all gone the ten men in the boat drew lots and ate the loser. They played the ghastly game again and again, until there were but two left—Captain George Pollard and a cabin boy. Just as Pollard contemplated killing the boy, another whaling vessel rescued them. From this episode came the Herman Melville classic *Moby Dick*.

The strangest story of Australian whaling—in fact the strangest sea tale since Jonah—is recorded in the ship's log of one of these whalers. In the year 1820, during the vessel's encounter with a whale, a sailor was thrown from the boat in the final struggle with the mammal and in the excitement was not missed.

When the fishermen were stripping the whale of its blubber they noticed a palpitation; they split open the belly and found the missing sailor, red in the face and unconscious but still alive. He had been inside the whale for nearly two hours. He said he remembered passing down a narrow passage, the walls nearly squeezing him to death but impelling him on into a large, noisome space; and then he fainted.

The whaling days at Twofold Bay, New South Wales, are now a matter of history, and with their passing, as at Sydney and Hobart, have closed a romantic and exciting chapter in the annals of that district.

There was a time when the quiet of the little township of Eden, overlooking Twofold Bay, on the South Coast of New South Wales, was often broken by the cry of 'Rush oh!' Men, women and children would scamper to vantage points on the adjacent cliffs commanding the bay and there watch the whalers put to sea. A whale chase was on, and this meant thrills, not only for the whalemen but for the onlookers.

The whalemen were assisted in their chases by a pack of remarkable mammals known as Killers or Killer Whales. The Killers were deadly enemies of the whales, and in the first week of June, as regularly as clockwork, they came from the Antarctic and took up their posts, like soldiers on guard, at the killer ground. This was an ocean rendezvous near the whaling station. They were all well known to the men and indeed each had his own name.

The Killers remained for about six months, patrolling the ocean. They were ever on the watch to turn a whale into the bay for the chasers. When a whale had been harpooned they 'assisted' in doing it to death. The Killers played the same part in whaling as sheep and cattle dogs play in droving. Immediately the harpoon was thrown, the Killers leapt over and over the impaled victim till he was completely exhausted. They drew off to permit the headman to drive the lance deep into the body of the whale; and then they prised open the mouth and dived in for their share—the tongue.

There died in the 1920s, at the age of 102, Mrs Euphemia Davidson, widow of John Davidson, of the Kiah River Whaling Station at Twofold Bay. So vanished one of the last of the original links with the old-time whalemen. The Davidsons were the leading folks amongst the whalemen, and it was said that the Killers refused to 'work' for crews other than those of the Davidsons. Since whaling ended at Twofold Bay the Killer pack has disappeared from the scene.

Some years later the carcase of one of them, Old Tom, was washed ashore, and his skeleton was preserved and can now be seen at Eden.

A story is told of George Davidson when on one occasion he was headman in Number One boat. He had just hurled the harpoon into a large whale when the attached rope fouled one of his legs, pulling him overboard into the depths. By frantic efforts the crew succeeded in letting out enough slack, and Davidson was able to free himself and rise to the surface some 200 yards (183 metres) away. He then calmly swam back to his boat, escorted in a protective sort of way by one of the Killers, Old Humpey. Only when he was pulled on board did the Killer turn and rejoin his mates in the chase.

A WHALE OF A SEA STORY
Some of the older generation of Australians have heard about the sinking of a vessel off Cape Leeuwin by a whale. The ship was the *Pet*, and thousands of youngsters have listened to the exciting story of how the whale charged the schooner and sent it to the bottom.

With bated breath they heard of how the captain went down with his ship and of the crew taking to the boat and rowing over to the lighthouse—all in broad daylight, in fine weather, and on a calm sea.

Many households once boasted a picture which represented the whale giving the schooner a wallop with its tail. In this picture, the whale faced the onlooker. Its great head was like that of a bulldog, with protruding eyes and a ferocious appearance. The sea, in the background, was disturbed, and littered with bits of the schooner. Other bits of her were high in the air. On the broken decks the crew of four was hoisting a boat in the tiny davits.

No doubt about it, the artist who drew that picture, though neither conversant with whales nor ships, had a vivid imagination—to say the least. But, if there were grave doubts as to his accuracy and marine qualifications, his subject was regarded as historical fact.

Time marched on. In the 1920s there died in Western Australia, one Bill Henrietta, who was mate of the schooner *Pet* at the time of her famous encounter. Bill had given up the sea and become a seasoned old landlubber; so much so that he was prospecting for gold around Coolgardie when he was an old man in his late seventies. Tall and broad-shouldered, his long, abundant beard and hair were silver grey. On his chest he sported the tattooed pattern of a ship in full sail. His great, hairy forearms showed designs in red and blue inks of flags and anchors and all the things dear to the heart of an old salt. His big, flat feet were obviously unspoiled by any confinement in leather. He rarely wore boots, and of the pair he possessed he admitted he didn't know the right from the left, and neither did the man who made them.

Old Bill often told of his whaling days—about all the sorts and sizes of whales and their tricks. He remembered each whale he'd harpooned. 'Some had died quietly, some had been contrary critters, others had broken loose and got away with a few hundred fathoms of line and a good harpoon, some had died straight and towed well to the whaling station, some had died with a kink in 'em, and even with a good wind you couldn't tow 'em at more than a knot an hour.'

It was all great stuff; told in an honest, effortless way without any boasting. When questioned, however, about the world famous epic in which the whale charged his schooner and sent her to the bottom of the sea, Bill was reticent. He'd dismiss the subject with 'Oh, you know the story. It's been told over and over again.'

But Bill Henrietta did tell the story—the true story—before he passed on. With advancing years, the old man's conscience evidently troubled him, and one day he unburdened himself to his intimate acquaintances (one of whom told me this tale). To use Bill's own words, 'The whale didn't charge the *Pet*. It was me who run the schooner up against the whale. She woke in a fright and bumped us. The mains'l jibed, the schooner heeled over, the cargo shifted, water poured into the open hatch, and down she went with the captain. He was asleep below.'

Bill then explained that, at the time of the occurrence, the schooner was on its way from Fremantle to Esperance Bay. He was at the helm when he saw the big whale asleep, almost on the ship's course. Fascinated by the sight of the great monster lying peacefully there, Bill put down the helm a bit, just to sail close to her and get a better view. But he came too close. The whale woke up in a fright. There was no room for her to turn, and she bumped the schooner. As he said, the mains'l jibed, gear shifted, and the vessel couldn't right herself. It was all over in a few moments.

Bill tried to wake the captain, but the water came down the companion-way before he could reach it. Bill and three of the crew scrambled clear and got the ship's boat over the rail just in time. They saw their ship sink, and then they rowed to the shore.

The men knew there would be a Marine Board inquiry—and that, if the facts came out, Bill Henrietta would be found guilty for the fatality. So it was that they agreed to tell the same story of how the whale had charged the ship. The world accepted that story as one of the wonder epics of the sea.

TRADITIONAL COLONIAL BALLADS

Transportation Ballads; Bushranging and Cattle Duffing Ditties; The Drovers;
Songs of the Shed; Days of the Diggings; The Swagmen; Immigrants;
Squatters and Selectors.

During the latter half of this century interest in the field of Australian colonial ballads has grown enormously. Prior to this the subject was largely ignored. To be sure, some of the rustic recitations that charmed our forefathers are often crude and maudlin, but they give us a picture of life in early colonial days as seen through the eyes of the ordinary man the drover, the digger, the shearer, the newly-arrived immigrant. We must remember that they were composed when our population was a curious conglomeration of highly-educated and ignorant people. Books and papers were luxuries, so ballad making came into vogue just as it had done in Europe centuries before.

All of the ballads in this selection (many of them have been in existence for well over a hundred years) are by anonymous writers with the exception of the first one—*Botany Bay*. Moreover, it is not a transportation song, although listed as such (it was written about 1885), but it is closely akin to a very old ditty on a similar theme called *Farewell to Judges and Juries*. The inclusion of *Botany Bay* is because of the fact that like *Waltzing Matilda* it has become accepted as part of Australia's traditional songs.

As ever with folk lore, there is not always complete agreement as to the text of some of the ballads. Thus *Sweet Alice (Dan Holt)* is also known under the title of *Sam Holt*; there are three known versions of *The Overlanders*, and several ballads have been woven around the adventures of the legendary *Billy Barlow*.

Examples from eight types or groups of ballads are shown in this chapter. They cover Transportation, Bushranging and Cattle Duffing, Droving, Songs of the Shed, On the Diggings, Swagmen, Immigrants, and Squatters and Selectors.

Transportation

Botany Bay

Farewell to old England for ever,
Farewell to my rum culls as well;
Farewell to the well-known old Bailee,
Where I used for to cut such a swell.

Chorus:
Singing too-ral li-oor-al li-ad-dity
Singing too-ral li-oor-al li-ay;
Singing too-ral li-oor-al li-ad-dity
Singing too-ral li-oor-al li-ay.

There's the Captain as is our Commander,
There's the bo'sun and all the ship's crew,
There's the first and second-class passengers,
Knows what we poor convicts go through.

'Taint leavin' old England we cares about,
'Taint cos we mispels what we knows,
But becos all we light-fingered gentry
Hops around with a log on our toes.

Oh, had I the wings of a turtle-dove!
I'd soar on my pinions so high,
Slap bang to the arms my Polly love,
And in her sweet presence I'd die.

Now, all my young Dookies and Duchesses,
Take warning from what I've to say,
Mind all is your own as you touchesses,
Or you'll find us in Botany Bay.

Jim Jones

Oh, listen for a moment, lads,
And hear me tell my tale;
How, over the sea from England's shore,
I was compelled to sail.
The jury says, 'He's guilty, sir!'
And says the judge, says he—
'For life, Jim Jones, I'm sending you
Across the stormy sea.

'And take my tip, before you ship
To join the iron gang,
Don't be too gay at Botany Bay,
Or else you'll surely hang.
Or else you'll hang,' he says, says he,
'And after that, Jim Jones,
High up upon the gallows tree
The crows will pick your bones.

'You'll have no chance for mischief then—
Remember what I say:
They'll flog the mischief out of you
When you get to Botany Bay!'

The waves were high upon the sea,
The winds blew up in gales;
I'd rather be drowned in misery
Than go to New South Wales.

For night and day the irons clang,
And, like poor galley slaves,
We toil and moil and when we die
Must fill dishonoured graves.
But by and by I'll break my chains
Into the bush I'll go;
And join the brave bushrangers there—
Jack Donahoe and Co.

And some dark night when everything
Is silent in the town,
I'll shoot the tyrants one and all
And shoot the floggers down.
I'll give the law a little shock—
Remember what I say.
They'll yet regret they sent Jim Jones
In chains to Botany Bay!

The Convicts' Rum Song

Cut yer name across me backbone,
Stretch me skin across a drum,
Iron me up on Pinchgut Island
From today till Kingdom Come!

*I will eat yer Norfolk dumpling**
Like a juicy Spanish plum,
Even dance the Newgate Hornpipe
If ye'll only gimme RUM!

* ('Norfolk dumpling': slang term for unpalatable food at the Norfolk Island penal settlement.)

BUSHRANGING AND CATTLE DUFFING

The Wild Colonial Boy

It's of a wild Colonial boy—Jack Dowling was his name:
Of poor but honest parents, he was born in Castlemaine.
He was his father's only son, his mother's pride and joy,
And dearly did they always love their wild Colonial boy.

Chorus:
Then come, all my hearties! We'll roam the mountains high;
Together we will plunder—together we will die!
We'll wander over valleys, and gallop over plains,
For we scorn to live in slavery, bound down with iron chains!

When scarcely sixteen years of age, Jack left his father's home,
And through Australia's sunny clime, a bushranger did roam.
He would rob the lordly squatters: their flocks he would destroy;
A terror to Australia was The Wild Colonial Boy!

In 'thirty-six this daring youth commenced his wild career,
With a heart that knew no danger; no foeman did he fear.
He stuck the Beechworth mail-coach up, and robbed, Judge McEvoy,
Who, trembling, gave his gold up to The Wild Colonial Boy.

He bade the judge 'Good morning', and told him to beware,
That he'd never rob 'an honest' judge who acted on the square.
But you would rob a mother of her son and only joy,
You'd breed a race of outlaws, like The Wild Colonial Boy!

As Jack rode out one morning, to view the scene around,
A-listening to the little birds, with their pleasant laughing sound,
Up rode three mounted troopers, Kelly, Davis and Fitzroy,
With a warrant for the capture of The Wild Colonial Boy.

'Surrender now, John Dowling—you see there's three to one;
Surrender in the Queen's name, you daring highwayman!'
Jack drew a pistol from his belt, and waved the little toy:
'I'll fight, but not surrender,' said The Wild Colonial Boy.

He fired at Trooper Kelly, and brought him to the ground,
But in return from Davis, received a mortal wound;
All shattered through the jaws he lay, still firing at Fitzroy—
And that is how they captured The Wild Colonial Boy.

Ballad of Ben Hall

Come all Australia's sons to me,
A hero has been slain,
Butchered by cowards in his sleep
Upon the Lachlan plain.
Ah, do not stay your seemly grief
But let the tear-drops fall,
Australian hearts will always mourn
The fate of Old Ben Hall.

He never robbed a needy man,
The records sure will show
How staunch and loyal to his mates,
How manly to his foe.
No brand of Cain e'er stamped his brow,
No widow's curse can fall:
Only the robber rich men feared
The coming of Ben Hall.

For ever since the good old days
Of Turpin and Duval,
The people's friends were outlaws,
And so was bold Ben Hall.
Yet savagely they murdered him,
Those coward blue-coat imps
Who only found his hiding place
From sneaking peelers' pimps.

Yes, savagely they murdered him;
Oh, let your tear-drops fall,
For all Australia mourns today
Her bravest son, Ben Hall.
No more he'll mount his gallant steed
To roam the ranges high;
Poor widow's friend in poverty,
Our bold Ben Hall, good-bye!

Bold Jack Donahoe

In Dublin town I was brought up, in that city of great fame—
My decent friends and parents, they will tell to you the same.
It was for the sake of five hundred pounds I was sent across the main,
For seven long years in New South Wales to wear a convict's chain

Chorus:
Then come, my hearties, we'll roam the mountains high!
Together we will plunder, together we will die!
We'll wander over mountains and we'll gallop over plains—
For we scorn to live in slavery, bound down in iron chains.

I'd scarce been there twelve months or more upon the Australian shore,
When I took to the highway, as I'd oft-times done before.
There was me and, Jacky Underwood, and Webber and Webster, too.
These were the true associates of bold Jack Donahoe.

Now Donahoe was taken, all for a notorious crime,
And sentenced to be hanged upon the gallows-tree so high.
But when they came to Sydney gaol he left them in a stew,
And when they came to call the roll they missed bold Donahoe.

As Donahoe made his escape, to the bush he went straightway.
The people they were all afraid to travel night or day—
For every week in the newspapers there was published something new
Concerning this dauntless hero, the bold Jack Donahoe!

As Donahoe was cruising, one summer's afternoon,
Little was his notion his death was near so soon,
When a sergeant of the horse police discharged his car-a-bine,
And called aloud on Donahoe to fight or to resign.

'Resign to you —you cowardly dog! a thing I ne'er will do,
For I'll fight this night with all my might,' cried bold Jack Donahoe.
'I'd rather roam these hills and dales, like wolf or kangaroo,
Than work one hour for government!' cried bold Jack Donahoe.

He fought six rounds with the horse police until the fatal ball,
Which pierced his heart and made him start, caused Donahoe to fall.
And as he closed his mournful eyes, he bade this world adieu,
Saying, 'Convicts all, both large and small, say prayers for Donahoe!'

(The convict bushranger Donahoe died in 1830. The chorus of this ballad is identical with the much later ballad, 'The Wild Colonial Boy'.)

The Ballad of Jack Power
(Air: 'Erin-go-Bragh')

'Twas the eighth day of August
 In the year sixty-nine,
On a lovely spring morning,
 The weather being fine,
When a bolter from Pentridge,
 Jack Power by name,
An aspirant for the gallows,
 To Beechworth he came.

Well armed, well mounted,
 The traps for his foes,
To the scrub for concealment
 The highwayman goes.
From Beechworth to the Buckland
 And on the highway
Run Cobb and Co's coaches
 By night and by day.

Early one morning
 The outlaw approached
Towards Bowman's forest
 And bail'd up the coach.
And he bail'd up two draymen,
 A new saddle stole
And a horse, a coach wheeler—
 It's true, by my soul!

He met with a trooper
  Near the small town of Yea—
'Good morning, Sir Trooper,
  My orders obey
Hand here that revolver
  Or, if you refuse,
You may fight or deliver,
  Pray, which do you choose?'

The trooper surrender'd
  His horse and his arms,
Then hastened to Yea town
  To give the alarm.
'Farewell', shouts the rover,
  'This revolver's my shield;
To the traps or the gallows
  I never will yield!'

We may sing of young Gilbert,
  Dan Morgan, Ben Hall,
But the bold reckless robber
  Surpasses them all.
The pluck that was in him
  Is beyond all belief—
A daring highwayman,
  A professional thief!

Dunn, Gilbert, and Ben Hall

Come! all ye lads of loyalty, and listen to my tale;
  A story of bushranging days, I will to you unveil,
'Tis of those gallant heroes, God bless them one and all,
  And we'll sit and sing: 'God save the Queen,
Dunn, Gilbert, and Ben Hall.'

To see the mounted troopers
  Scouring the bush,
Like diggers in the olden times,
  Hasting to a rush;

But those bushranging heroes
  They do deceive them all,
There's one thousand pounds, alive or dead,
  For Dunn, Gilbert, or Ben Hall.

As Ben was riding out one day,
  His trade being rather slack,
By private information
  The troops got on his track,
Saying, 'Hall, you are my prisoner,
  Surrender unto me,'
And Ben bolted from his saddle
  And climbed up in a tree.

With rage and disappointment
  The troopers cursed and swore;
They moped and poked about the bush,
  And tracked him o'er and o'er;
They kept the watch till daylight,
  And no Ben could be found;
At length they saw his cabbage-tree*
  A-lying on the ground.

Then away goes eight or ten of them,
  Like so many yelping curs,
To capture bold Morgan.†
  In his shining boots and spurs;
But the horses, they knocked up at last,
  He cannot captured be;
They turned back from a fruitless chase,
  And Morgan still is free.

*Cabbage-tree: Cabbage-tree hat.
† Daniel Morgan, contemporary bushranger of Ben Hall, but not one of his gang.

The troopers now, in latter days,
    They're only paper men,
Not like the mounted heroes
    We had in thirty-nine;
But a man that's carrying on the road
    Is taken from his dray,
With a pair of bracelets on his wrists,
    He's captured—led away.

So now my song is ended,
    I think I will resign,
We'll toast those gallant heroes
    In a glass of sparkling wine;
We'll give them three times three, my boys,
    We'll toast them one and all,
And we'll sit and sing 'Long live the Queen,
    Dunn, Gilbert, and Ben Hall.'

The Eumerella Shore
A Cattle Duffers' Song

There's a happy little valley on the Eumerella shore,
    Where I've lingered many happy hours away,
On my little free selection I have acres by the score,
    Where I unyoke the bullocks from the dray.

Chorus:
To my bullocks then I say
No matter where you stray,
    You will never be impounded any more;
For you're running, running, running on the duffer's piece of land,
    Free selected on the Eumerella shore.

When the moon has climbed the mountains and the stars are shining
        bright,
    Then we saddle up our horses and away,
And we steal the squatters' cattle in the darkness of the night,
    And we brand 'em at the dawning of the day.

Chorus:
Oh, my little poddy calf,
At the squatter you may laugh,
*   For he'll never be your owner any more;*
For you're running, running, running on the duffer's piece of land,
*   Free selected on the Eumeralla shore.*

If we find a mob of horses when the paddock rails are down,
*   Although before, they've never known to stray,*
Oh, quickly will we drive them to some distant inland town,
*   And sell them into slav'ry far away.*

Chorus:
To Jack Robertson we'll say
You've been leading us astray,
*   And we'll never go a-farming any more;*
For it's easier duffing cattle on the little piece of land
*   Free selected on the Eumerella shore.*

('Duffing': Like the American term 'rustling'—the thieving of cattle and horses. 'Jack Robertson': John, later Sir John Robertson, New South Wales Premier who introduced the 1861 Land Act to assist small farmers. Instead, it consolidated the big land-holders.)

IMMIGRANTS

Paddy Malone in Australia

Och! my name's Pat Malone, and I'm from Tipperary,
*   Sure, I don't know it now, I'm so bothered, Ohone!*
And the gals that I danced with light-hearted and airy,
*   It's scarcely they'd notice poor Paddy Malone.*
'Tis twelve months or more since our ship she cast anchor
*   In happy Australia, the emigrant's home,*
And from that day to this there's been nothing but canker,
*   And grafe and vexation for Paddy Malone.*
Oh, Paddy Malone! Oh, Paddy Ohone!
*   Bad luck to the agent that coaxed ye to roam.*

Wid a man called a squatter I soon got a place, sure;
    He'd a beard like a goat, and such whiskers, Ohone!
And he said—as he peeped through the hair on his faitures—
    That he liked the appearance of Paddy Malone.
Wid him I agreed to go up to his station,
    Saying 'Abroad in the bush you'll find yourself at home',
I liked his proposal, and wi'out hesitation
    Signed my name wid a X that spelt Paddy Malone.
Oh, Paddy Malone, you're no scholard, Ohone!
    Sure, I made a criss-crass that spell Paddy Malone.

A-herding my sheep in the bush, as they call it—
    It was no bush at all, but a mighty great wood,
Wid all the big trees that were small bushes one time,
    A long time ago, faith! I 'spose fore the flood.
To find out this big bush one day I went further,
    The trees grew so thick that I couldn't, Ohone!
I tried to go back then, but that I found harder,
    And bothered and lost was poor Paddy Malone.
Oh, Paddy Malone, through the bush he did roam!
    What a babe in the wood was poor Paddy Malone.

I was soon overcome, sure, wid grafe and vexation,
    And camped, you must know, by the side of a log;
I was found the next day by a man from the station,
    For I coo-eed and roared like a bull in a bog.
The man said to me, 'Arrah, Pat! where's the sheep now?'
    Says I, 'I dunno! barring one here at home,'
And the master began and kicked up a big row, too,
    And swore he'd stop the wages of Paddy Malone.
Arrah! Paddy Malone, you're no shepherd, Ohone!
    We'll try you with bullocks now, Paddy Malone.

To see me dressed out with my team and my dray too,
    Wid a whip like a flail and such gaiters, Ohone!
But the bullocks, they eyed me, and seemed for to say, too,
    'You may do your best, Paddy, we're blest if we go.'
'Gee whoa! Redman! Come hither, Damper!
    Hoot, Magpie! Gee, Blackbird! Come hither, Whalebone!'

But the brutes turned round sharp, and away thy did scamper,
  And heels over head turned poor Paddy Malone.
Oh, Paddy Malone! You've seen some bulls at home,
  But the bulls of Australia cow Paddy Malone.

I was found the next day where the brutes thy did throw me
  By a man passing by, upon hearing me groan;
And, wiping the mud from my face till he knew me,
  Says he, 'Your name's Paddy? Yes! Paddy Malone,'
I thin says to him, 'You're an angel sent down, sure!'
  'No, faith, but I'm not; but a friend of your own!'
And by his persuasion, for home then I started,
  And you now see before you poor Paddy Malone.
Arrah, Paddy Malone! you are now safe at home.
  Bad luck to the agent that coaxed ye to roam.

Colonial Experience
('Air: 'So Early in the Morning')

When first I came to Sydney Cove
And up and down the streets did rove,
I thought such sights I ne'er did see
Since first I learnt my A B C.

Chorus:
Oh! it's broiling in the morning,
It's toiling in the morning,
It's broiling in the morning,
It's toiling all day long.

Into the park I took a stroll—
I felt just like a buttered roll.
A pretty name 'The Sunny South!'
A better one 'The Land of Drouth!'

Next day into the bush I went,
On wild adventure I was bent,
Dame Nature's wonders I'd explore,
All thought of danger would ignore.

The mosquitoes and bull-dog ants
Assailed me even through my pants.
It nearly took my breath away
To hear the jackass laugh so gay!

This lovely country, I've been told,
Abounds in silver and in gold.
You may pick it up all day,
Just as leaves in autumn lay!

Marines will chance this yarn believe,
But blue jackets you can't deceive.
Such pretty stories will not fit,
Nor can I their truth admit.

Some say there's lots of work to do.
Well, yes, but then, 'twixt me and you,
A man may toll and broil all day—
The big, fat man gets all the pay.

Mayhap such good things there may be,
But you may have them all, for me,
Instead of roaming foreign parts
I wish I'd studied the Fine Arts!

The Bushman's Lullaby

Lift me down to the creek-bank, Jack;
It must be cooler outside;
The long hot day is well-nigh done,
It's a chance if I see another one.
I should like to look on the setting sun,
And the waters cool and wide.

We didn't think it would be like this
Last week as we rode together;
True mates we've been in this far land
For many a day since Devon's strand
We left for these wastes of sun-scorched land,
In the blessed English weather.

We left when the leafy lanes were green,
And the trees met overhead;
The merry brooks ran clear and gay;
The air was sweet with the scent of hay;
How well I remember the very day,
And the words my mother said.

We have striven and toiled and fought it out
Under the hard blue sky,
Where the plains glowed red in tremulous light,
Where the haunting mirage mocked the sight
Of desperate men from morn till night,
And the streams had long been dry.

Where we dug for gold on the mountain side,
Where the ice-fed river ran,
Through frost and blast, through fire and snow,
Where an Englishman could live and go,
We've followed our luck for weal or woe,
And never asked help from man.

And now it's over, it's hard to die,
Ere the summer of life is o'er,
Ere time has printed one single mark,
When the pulse beats high, and the limbs are stark,
And, oh God, to see home no more!

No more! No more! Ah! vain the vow,
That, whether rich or poor,
Whatever the years might bring or change,
I would one day stand by the grey old grange
While the children gathered, all shy and strange,
As I entered the well-known door.

You will go home to the old place, Jack;
Tell my mother from me
That I thought of the words she used to say,
Her looks, her tone, as I dying lay;
That I prayed to God as I used to pray
When I knelt beside her knee.

By the lonely water thy made their couch,
And the southern night fast fled;
They heard the wild fowl splash and cry,
They heard the mourning reeds low sigh.
Such was the bushman's lullaby;
With the dawn his soul was sped.

SQUATTERS AND SELECTORS

The Squatter's Man

'Come, all ye lads an' list to me,
That's left your homes an' crossed the sea
To try your fortune, bound or free,
    All in this golden land.
For twelve long months I had to pace,
Humping my swag with a cadging face,
Sleeping in the bush, like the sable race,
    As in my song you'll understand.

Unto this country I did come,
A regular out-and-out new chum.
I then abhorred the sight of rum—
    Teetotal was my plan.
But soon I learned to wet one eye—
Misfortune oft-times made me sigh.
To raise fresh funds I was forced to fly,
    And be a squatter's man.

Soon at a station I appeared.
I saw the squatter with his beard,
And up to him I boldly steered
 With my swag and billy-can.
I said, 'Kind sir, I want a job!'
Said he, 'Do you know how to snob,
Or can you break in a bucking cob?'
 Whilst my figure he well did scan.

' 'Tis now I want a useful cove
To stop at home and not to rove.
The scams go about—a regular drove—
 I suppose you're one of the clan?
But I'll give you ten, ten, sugar an' tea;
Ten bob a week, if you'll suit me,
And very soon I hope you'll be
 A handy squatter's man.

'At daylight you must milk the cows,
Make butter, cheese, an' feed the sows,
Put on the kettle, the cook arouse,
 And clean the family shoes.
The stable an' sheep yard clean out,
And always answer when we shout,
With 'Yes, ma'am', and 'No, sir'; mind your mouth,
 And my youngsters don't abuse.

'You must fetch wood an' water, bake an' boil,
Act as butcher when we kill;
The corn an' taters you must hill,
 Keep the garden spic and span.
You must not scruple in the rain
To take to market all the grain.
Be sure you come sober back again
 To be a squatter's man.'

He sent me to an old bark hut,
Inhabited by a greyhound slut,
Who put her fangs through my poor fut,
    And, snarling, off she ran.
So once more I'm looking for a job,
Without a copper in my fob.
With Ben Hall or Gardener I'd rather rob,
    Than be a squatter's man.

The New England Cocky*

'Twas a New England cocky, as of late I've been told,
Who died, so 'tis said, on account of the cold;
When dying, he called to his children 'Come here!
As I'm dying, I want my fortune to share.

'Dear children, you know I've toiled early and late,
I've struggled with nature, and wrestled with fate.
Then all do your best to my fortune repair;
And to my son John I leave a dear native bear.

'To Mary I give my pet kangaroo,
May it prove to turn out a great blessing, too.,
To Michael I leave the old cockatoo,
And to Bridget I'll give the piebald emu.

'To the others whatever is left I will leave—
Don't quarrel, or else my poor spirit will grieve;
There's the fish in the stream, and the fowl on the lake,
Let each have as much as any may take.

'And now, my dear children, no more can I do,
My fortune I've fairly divided with you,'
And these were the last words his children did hear—
'Don't forget that I reared you on pumpkin and bear.'

(Cocky: A small farmer or settler. The term is said to have been derived from cockatoo farmer—one who works hard, fencing, ploughing, and sowing his small selection only to see the ground white with cockatoos grubbing up his seed.)

The Free Selector

Ye sons of industry, to you I belong,
And to you I would dedicate a verse or a song.
Rejoicing o'er the victory John Robertson has won
Now the Land Bill has passed and the good time has come.

No more with our swags through the bush need we roam
For to ask of another there to give us a home;
Now the land is unfettered, and we may reside
In a home of our own by some clear waterside.

On some fertile spot which we may call our own,
Where the rich verdure grows we will build up a home;
There industry will flourish and content will smile,
While our children rejoicing will share in our toil.

We will plant our garden and sow our own field,
And eat from the fruits which industry will yield,
And be independent, as long we have strived,
Though those that have ruled us the right long denied.

Jimmy Sago, Jackeroo
(Air: 'Wearing of the Green')

If you want a situation, I'll just tell you the plan
To get on to a station, I'm just your very man.
Pack up the old portmanteau, and label it Paroo,
With a name aristocratic—Jimmy Sago, Jackeroo.

When you get on to the station, of small things you'll make a fuss,
And in speaking of the station, mind, it's we, and ours, and us.
Boast of your grand connections and your rich relations, too,
And your own great expectations, Jimmy Sago, Jackeroo.

They will send you out on horseback, the boundaries to ride;
But run down a marsupial and rob him of his hide,
His scalp will fetch a shilling and his hide another two,
Which will help to fill your pockets, Jimmy Sago, Jackeroo.
Yes, to fill your empty pockets, Jimmy Sago, Jackeroo.

When the boss wants information, on the men you'll do a sneak,
And don a paper collar on your fifteen bob a week.
Then at the lamb-marking a boss they'll make of you.
Now that's the way to get on, Jimmy Sago, Jackeroo.

A squatter in the future I've no doubt you may be,
But if the banks once get you, they'll put you up a tree.
To see you humping bluey, I know, would never do,
'Twould mean good-bye to our new chum, Jimmy Sago, Jackeroo.
Yes, good-bye to our new chum, Jimmy Sago, Jackeroo.

(A jackeroo of the early days was usually a young Englishman or a young Australian townsman working on a station to gain experience. They were often unpopular with station hands and shearers because they were supposedly 'favoured workers' and regarded as being on a higher social plane than the others.)

Billy Barlow in Australia

(This bush song appeared on the programme of the Maitland Amateur Company's Benevolent Society's performance in the 'long room' of the Northumberland Hotel, West Maitland, NSW, on 28th August 1843. The story of Billy Barlow is typical of the times. A convict, after serving part of his sentence, could qualify for a 'ticket-of-leave' pass. This was his protection when accosted by a trooper. But a free immigrant had no such protection and was always liable to be arrested on suspicion of being an escaped convict.)

When I was at Home I was down on my luck,
And earned a poor living by drawing a truck;
But old aunt died, and left me a thousand— 'Oh, Oh!
I'll start on my travels,' thought Billy Barlow.
    Oh, dear, lack-a-day, oh!
    So of to Australia came Billy Barlow.

When to Sydney I got, there a merchant I met,
Who said he would teach me a fortune to get;
He'd cattle and sheep past the Colony's bounds,
Which he sold with a station for my thousand pounds.
    Oh, dear, lack-a-day, oh!
    He gammoned the cash out of Billy Barlow.

When the bargain was struck, and the money was paid,
He said, 'My dear fellow, your fortune is made;
I can furnish supplies for the station you know,
And your bill is sufficient, dear Mr Barlow!'
    Oh, dear, lack-a-day, oh!
    A gentleman settler was Billy Barlow.

So I got my supplies, and I gave him my bill,
And for New England started, my pockets to fill;
But by bushrangers met, with my traps they made free,
Took my horse, and left Billy tied up to a tree.
    Oh, dear, lack-a-day, oh!
    'I'll die of starvation,' thought Billy Barlow.

At last I got loose, and I walked on my way;
A trooper came up, and to me did say:
'Are you free?' Says I, 'Yes to be sure; don't you know?'
And I handed my card— 'Mr William Barlow.'
    Oh, dear, lack-a-day, oh!
    He said, 'That's all gammon,' to Billy Barlow.

Then he put on the handcuffs, and brought me away,
Right back down to Maitland, before Mr Day.
When I said I was free, why the J.P. replied:
'I must send you to Sydney to be identified.'
    Oh, dear, lack-a-day, oh!
    So to Sydney once more went poor Billy Barlow.

They at last let me go, and I then did repair
For my station once more, and at length I got there;
But a few days before, the blacks, you must know,
Had speared all the cattle of Billy Barlow.
    Oh, dear, lack-a-day, oh!
    'It's a beautiful country,' said Billy Barlow.

And for nine months before, no rain there had been,
So the devil a blade of grass could be seen;
And one-third of my wethers the scab they had got,
And the other two-thirds had just died of the rot.
    Oh, dear, lack-a-day, oh!
    'I shall soon be a settler,' said Billy Barlow.

And the matter to mend, now my bill was near due,
So I wrote to my friend, and asked him to renew;
He replied he was sorry he couldn't, because
The bill had passed into a usurer's claws.
    Oh, dear, lack-a-day, oh!
    'But perhaps he'll renew it,' thought Billy Barlow.

I applied; to renew he was oh! so content,
If secured, and allowed just three hundred per cent;
But as I couldn't do, Barr, Rodgers and Co.
Quick sent up a summons for Billy Barlow.

Oh, dear, lack-a-day, oh!
They settled the hash of poor Billy Barlow.

For a month or six weeks I stewed over my loss,
When a tall man rode up one day on a black horse;
He asked, 'Don't you know me?' I answered him 'No.'
'Why,' said he, 'My name's Kingsmill. How are you, Barlow?'
   Oh, dear, lack-a-day, oh!
   He'd got a 'Fi. fa.' for poor Billy Barlow.

What I'd left of my sheep and my traps he did seize,
And he said, 'They won't pay all the costs and MY FEES';
Then he sold off the lot, and I'm sure 'twas a sin,
At sixpence a head, and the station thrown in.
   Oh, dear, lack-a-day, oh!
   'I'll go back to England,' said Billy Barlow.

My sheep being sold, and my money all gone,
Oh! I wandered about then quite sad and forlorn,
How I managed to live, it would shock you to know,
And as thin as a lath got poor Billy Barlow.
   Oh, dear, lack-a-day, oh!
   Quite down on his luck was poor Billy Barlow.

In a few further weeks, the Sheriff, you see,
Sent a tall man on horseback once more unto me;
Having got all he could by the writ of 'Fi. fa.',
By way of a change he'd brought up a 'Ca. sa.'
   Oh, dear, lack-a-day, oh!
   He seized on the body of Billy Barlow.

He took me to Sydney, and there they did lock
Poor unfortunate Billy fast 'under the clock';
And to get myself out I was forced, you must know,
The schedule to file of poor Billy Barlow.
   Oh, dear, lack-a-day, oh!
   In the list of insolvents was Billy Barlow.

SWAGMEN

The Swagman

Kind friends, pray give attention
  To this, my little song.
Some rum things I will mention,
  And I'll not detain you long.
Up and down this country
  I travel, don't you see,
I'm a swagman on the wallaby,
  Oh! don't you pity me.
I'm a swagman on the wallaby,
  Oh! don't you pity me.

At first I started shearing,
  And I bought a pair of shears.
On my first sheep appearing,
  Why, I cut off both its ears.
Then I nearly skinned the brute,
  As clean as clean could be.
So I was kicked out of the shed,
  Oh! don't you pity me. (etc.)

I started station loafing,
  Short stages and took my ease;
So all day long till sundown
  I'd camp beneath the trees.
Then I'd walk up to the station,
  The manager to see.
'Boss, I'm hard up and I want a job,
  Oh! don't you pity me.' (etc.)

Says the overseer: 'Go to the hut,
  In the morning I'll tell you
If I've any work about
  I can find for you to do.'
But at breakfast I cuts off enough
  For dinner, don't you see

And then my name is Walker.
  Oh! don't you pity me.
I'm a swagman (etc.)

And now, my friends, I'll say good-bye,
  For I must go and camp.
For if the Sergeant sees me
  He may take me for a tramp;
But if there's any covey here
  What's got a cheque, d'ye see,
I'll stop and help him smash it.
  Oh! don't you pity me.
I'm a swagman on the wallaby,
  Oh! don't you pity me.

My Four Little Johnny-Cakes

Hurrah for the Lachlan, boys, and join me in a cheer;
That's the place to go to make a cheque every year.
With a toadskin in my pocket, that I borrowed from a friend,
Oh, isn't it nice and cosy to be camping in the bend!

Chorus:
With my four little johnny-cakes all nicely cooked,
A nice little codfish just off the hook;
My little round flour-bag sitting on a stump,
My little tea-and-sugar bag a-looking nice and plump.

I have a loaf of bread and some murphies that I shook,
Perhaps a loaf of brownie that I snavelled of the cook,
A nice leg of mutton, just a bit cut off the end,
Oh, isn't it nice and jolly to be whaling in the bend!

I have a little book and some papers for to read,
Plenty of matches and a good supply of weed:
I envy not the squatter, as at my fire I sit,
With a paper in my hand and my old clay a-lit.

And when the shearing-time comes round, I'm in my glory then;
I saddle up my moke and then secure a pen;
I canter thro' the valley, and gallop o'er the plain;
I shoot a turkey or stick a pig, and off to camp again.

(Toadskin: a five-pound note. Murphies: potatoes. Whaling: a tramplike, idle life along the banks of a river. Weed: tobacco.)

The Ramble-eer

The earth rolls on through empty space, it's journey's never done;
It's entered for a starry race throughout the kingdom come;
And, as I am a bit of earth, I follow it because—
And to prove I am a rolling stone and never gather moss.

Chorus:
For I a a ramble-eer, a rollicking ramble-eer,
I'm a roving rake of poverty, and son of a gun for beer.

I've done a bit of fossicking for tucker and for gold;
I've been a menial rouseabout and a rollicking shearer bold;
I've 'shanked' across the Old Man Plain, after busting up a cheque,
And 'whipped the cat' once more again, though I haven't met it yet.

I've done a bit of droving of cattle and of sheep
And I've done a bit of moving with 'Matilda' for a mate;
Of fencing I have done my share, wool-scouring on the green,
Axeman, navvy; Old Nick can bear me out in what I haven't been.

I've worked the treadmill thresher, the scythe and reaping-hook,
Been wood-and-water fetcher for Mary Jane the cook;
I've done a few 'cronk' things, too, when I have struck a town,
There's few things I wouldn't do—but I never did 'lambing down'.

('whip the cat:' crying over spilt milk. 'Matilda': swag. 'cronk': bad, poor. 'lambing down': encouraging a man to spend all his money on liquor.)

The Old Bark Hut

Oh my name is Bob the Swagman, before you all I stand,
And I've had many ups and downs while travelling through the land.
I once was well-to-do, my boys, but now I am stumped up,
And I'm forced to go on rations in an old bark hut.

Chorus:
In an old bark hut. In an old bark hut.
I'm forced to go on rations in an old bark hut.

Ten Pounds of flour, ten pounds of beef, some sugar and some tea,
That's all they give to a hungry man, until the Seventh Day.
If you don't be moighty sparing, you'll go with a hungry gut—
For that's one of the great misfortunes in an old bark hut.

Chorus:
In an old bark hut. In an old bark hut.
For that's one of the great misfortunes in an old bark hut.

The bucket you boil your beef in has to carry water, too,
And they'll say you're getting mighty flash if you should ask for two.
I've a billy, and a pint pot, and a broken-handled cup,
And they all adorn the table in the old bark hut.

Chorus:
In the old bark hut. In the old bark hut.
And they all adorn the table in the old bark hut.

Faith, the table is not made of wood, as many you have seen—
For if I had one half so good, I'd think myself serene—

'Tis only an old sheet of bark—God knows when it was cut—
It was blown from off the rafters of the old bark hut.

Chorus:
In an old bark hut. In an old bark hut.
It was blown from off the rafters of the old bark hut.

And of furniture, there's no such thing, 'twas never in the place,
Except the stool I sit upon—and that's an old gin case.
It does us for a safe as well, but you must keep it shut,
Or the flies would make it canter round the old bark hut.

Chorus:
In an old bark hut. In an old bark hut.
Or the flies would make it canter round the old bark hut.

If you should leave it open, and the flies should find your meat,
They'll scarcely leave a single piece that's fit for man to eat.
But you mustn't curse nor grumble—what won't fatten will fill up—
For what's out of sight is out of mind in an old bark hut.

Chorus:
In an old bark hut. In an old bark hut.
For what's out of sight is out of mind in an old bark hut.

In the summer time, when the weather's warm, this hut is nice and cool,
And you'll find the gentle breezes blowing in through every hole.
You can leave the old door open, or you can leave it shut,
There's no fear of suffocation in the old bark hut.

Chorus:
In an old bark hut. In an old bark hut.
There's no fear of suffocation in the old bark hut.

In the winter time—preserve us all!—to live in there's a treat,
Especially when it's raining hard, and blowing wind and sleet.
The rain comes down the chimney, and your meat is black with soot—
That's a substitute for pepper in an old bark hut.

Chorus:
In an old bark hut. In an old bark hut.
That's a substitute for pepper in an old bark hut.

I've seen the rain come in this hut just like a perfect flood,
Especially through that great big hole where once the table stood.
There's not a blessed spot, me boys, where you could lay your nut,
But the rain is sure to find you in the old bark hut.

Chorus:
In an old bark hut. In an old bark hut.
But the rain is sure to find you in the old bark hut.

So beside the fire I make me bed, and there I lay me down,
And think myself as happy as the king that wears a crown.
But as you'd be dozing of to sleep a flea will wake you up,
Which makes you curse the vermin in the old bark hut.

Chorus:
In an old bark hut. In an old bark hut.
Which makes you curse the vermin in the old bark hut.

Faith, such flocks of fleas you never saw, they are so plump and fat,
And if you make a grab at one, he'll spit just like a cat.
Last night they got my pack of cards, and were fighting for the cut—
I thought the devil had me in the old bark hut.

Chorus:
In an old bark hut. In an old bark hut.
I thought the devil had me in the old bark hut.
So now, my friends, I've sung my song, and that as well as I could,
And I hope the ladies present won't think my language rude,
And all ye younger people, in the days when you grow up,
Remember Bob the Swagman, and the old bark hut.

Chorus:
In an old bark hut. In an old bark hut.
Remember Bob the Swagman, and the old bark hut.

Click go the Shears

Down by the pen the old shearer stands,
Grasping the shears in his thin bony hands,
Fixed is his gaze on a bare bellied joe,
If he gets another one, oh Lord, won't he blow!

Chorus:
Click go the shears, boys, Click! Click! Click!
Wide is his blow, and his hands move quick.
The ringer looks around and is beaten by a blow,
And curses the old codger with the bare bellied joe.

In the middle of the floor in his cane bottom chair
Sits the boss of the board with his eyes everywhere.
Notes well each fleece as it comes to the screen,
Paying strict attention that it's taken off clean.

The tar boy is there, waiting in demand,
With his blacken'd tar pot and his tarry hands.
See one old sheep with a cut upon its back,
Here's what he's waiting for, it's 'Tar here, Jack!'

Shearing is all over and we've all got our cheques,
So it's roll up your swags, boys, we're off to the next.
The first pub we come to we'll all have a spree,
And everyone who comes along, it's come and drink with me.

Down by the bar the old shearer stands,
Grasping his glass in his thin bony hands.
Fixed is his gaze on a green painted keg,
Glory, he'll get down on it, ere he stirs a leg.

The Banks of the Condamine

Oh, hark the dogs are barking, love, I can no longer stay,
The men are all gone mustering, and it is nearly day;
And I must off by the morning, before the sun doth shine,
To meet the Sydney shearers on the banks of the Condamine.

Oh Willie, dearest Willie, I'll go along with you,
I'll cut of all my auburn fringe and be a shearer, too.
I'll cook and count your tally, love, while ringer-o you shine,
And I'll wash your greasy moleskins on the banks of the Condamine.

Oh, Nancy, dearest Nancy, with me you cannot go,
The squatters have given orders, love, no woman should do so;
Your delicate constitution is not equal unto mine,
To stand the constant tigering on the banks of the Condamine.

Oh Willie, dearest Willie, then stay back home with me,
We'll take up a selection, and a farmer's wife I'll be;
I'll help you husk the corn, love, and cook your meals so fine
You'll forget the ram-stag mutton on the banks of the Condamine.

Oh Nancy, dearest Nancy, please do not hold me back,
Down there the boys are waiting, and I must be on the track;
So here's a good-bye kiss, love, back home here I'll incline,
When we've shore the last of the jum-bucks on the banks of the Condamine.

Another Fall of Rain
(Air: 'Little Low Log Cabin in the Lane')

The weather had been sultry for a fortnight's time or more,
And the shearers had been driving might and main,
For some had got the century who'd ne'er got it before,
And now all hands were wishing for the rain.

Chorus:
For the boss is getting rusty, and the ringer's caving in,
For his bandaged wrist is aching with the pain,

And the second man, I fear, will make it hot for him,
    Unless we have another fall of rain.

A few had taken quarters, and were coiling in their bunks
    When we shore the six-tooth wethers from the plain.
And if the sheep get harder, then a few more men will funk,
    Unless we get another fall of rain.

But the sky is clouding over, and the thunder's muttering loud,
    And the clouds are driving eastward o'er the plain,
And I see the lightning flashing from the edge of yon black cloud,
    And I hear the gentle patter of the rain.

So lads, put on your stoppers, and let us to the hut,
    Where we'll gather round and have a friendly game,
While some are playing music and some play ante up,
    And some are gazing outwards at the rain.

But now the rain is over; let the pressers spin the screw,
    Let the teamsters back the wagons in again,
And we'll block the chaser's table by the way we'll put them through
    For everything is merry since the rain.

And the boss he won't be rusty when his sheep they are all shorn,
    And the ringer's wrist won't ache much with the pain
Of pocketing his cheque for fifty pounds or more,
    And the second man will press him hard again.

(The strain of shearing by the old hand-clippers is very severe on wrists. The ringer, or fastest shearer, would be apt to go in the wrists, especially early in the season. Hence the hope of the shearers for a fall of rain after a long dry spell.)

Widgeegowera Joe
(Air: 'Castle Gardens')

I'm only a back-blocks shearer, as easily can be seen,
I've shore in almost every shed on the plains of Riverine;
I've shore in most of the famous sheds, I've seen big tallies done,
But somehow or other, I don't know why, I never became a gun.

Chorus:
Hurrah, my boys, my shears are set, I feel both fit and well,
Tomorrow you'll find me at my pen when the gaffer rings the bell;
With Hayden's patent thumb-guards fixed, and both my blades pulled back,
Tomorrow I go with my sardine blow for a century or the sack.

I've opened up the windpipe straight, I've opened behind the ear;
I've practised every possible style in which a man can shear.
I've studied all the cuts and drives of the famous men I've met,
But I've never succeeded in plastering up them three little figures yet.

As the boss walked down this morning, I saw him stare at me.
For I'd mastered Moran's great shoulder cut, as he could plainly see;
But I've another surprise for him, that'll give his nerves a shock,
Tomorrow he'll find that I have mastered Pierce's rang-tank block.

And if I succeed as I expect to do, then I intend to shear
At the Wagga demonstration, which is held there every year;
And there I'll lower the colours, the colours of Mitchell and Co.,
Instead of Deeming, you will hear of Widgeegowera foe.

('I never became a gun': A big-gun shearer—one with an outstanding tally of sheep shorn in a day's work. Moran and Pierce were two such champions. Deeming (last line) refers to the notorious mass-murderer then in the news.)

The Sheep Washer's Lament
(Air: 'The Bonnie Irish Boy')

Come now, ye sighing washers all,
*   Join in my doleful lay,*
Mourn for the times none can recall,
*   With hearts to grief a prey.*
We'll mourn the washer's sad downfall
*   In our regretful strain,*
Lamenting on the days gone by
*   Ne'er to return again.*

When first I went a-washing sheep
*   The year was sixty-one,*
The master was a worker then,
*   The servant was a man;*
But now the squatters, puffed with pride,
*   They treat us with disdain;*
Lament the days that are gone by
*   Ne'er to return again.*

From sixty-one to sixty-six
*   The bushman, stout and strong,*
Would smoke his pipe and whistle his tune,
*   And sing his cheerful song,*
As wanton as the kangaroo
*   That bounds across the plain.*
Lament the days that are gone by
*   Ne'er to return again.*

Supplies of food unstinted, good,
*   No squatter did withhold.*
With plenty grog to cheer our hearts,
*   We feared nor heat nor cold,*
With six-and-six per man per day
*   We sought not to complain.*
Lament the days that are gone by
*   Ne'er to return again.*

With perfect health, a mine of wealth,
  Our days seemed short and sweet,
On pleasure bent our evenings spent,
  Enjoyment was complete.
But now we toil from morn till night,
  Though much against the grain,
Lamenting on the days gone by,
  Ne'er to return again.

May bushmen all in unity
  Combine with heart and hand,
May cursed, cringing poverty
  Be banished from the land.
In Queensland may prosperity
  In regal glory reign,
And washers in the time to come
  Their vanished rights regain.

The Big-Gun Shearer
(A Song of the Sheep Shearing-by-Hand Days)

Now, some shearing I have done, and some prizes I have won,
Through my knuckling down so close on the skin;
But I'd rather 'Tommyhock' every day and shear a flock,
For that's the only way to make some tin!

Chorus:
I am just about to cut out for the Darling:
To turn a hundred out I know the plan;
Give me sufficient cash, and you'll see me make a splash,
For I'm Tomahawking Fred, the ladies' man!

Put me on a shearing floor, and it's there I'm game to bet,
That I'd give to any ringer ten sheep start;
When on the whipping side, away from them I slide,
Just like a bullet or a dart.

Of me you might have read, for I'm Tomahawking Fred,
My shearing laurels known both near and far;
I'm the Don of Riverine, 'midst the shearers cut a shine;
And the tar-boys say I never call for tar.

Wire in and go ahead, for I'm Tomahawking Fred;
In a shearing shed, my lads, I cut a shine.
What of Roberts and Jack Gunn—shearing laurels they have won,
But my tally's never under ninety-nine.

DROVING

The Overlander

There's a trade you all know well,
It's bringing cattle over;
On every track to the Gulf and back
They know the Queensland drover.

Chorus:
Pass the billy round, my boys,
    Don't let the pint pots stand there,
For tonight we'll drink the health
    Of every Overlander.

Oh, I'm a bushman bold,
    Since youth I've been a rover;
On every track to the Gully and back
    They know McVeigh the drover.

I come from northern plains
    Where grass and girls is scanty,
Where the creeks run dry or ten feet high,
    And it's either drought or plenty.

A girl in Sydney town
    Said, 'Please don't leave me lonely';
I said, 'I'm sad, but my old prad
    Has room for one man only.'

I never stole a shirt
    As all my mates can say,
Unless I passed a town
    Up on a washing day.

Those little brats of kids,
    My God, they get my dander,
Singing, 'Ma, bring in the clothes,
    Here comes an Overlander!'

And now we're jogging back;
    This old nag she's a doer;
We'll pick up a job with a crawling mob
    Somewhere on the Maranoa.

A Thousand Miles Away
(Air: 'Ten Thousand Miles Away')

Hurrah for the Roma railway! Hurrah for Cobb and Co.,
And oh! for a good fat horse or two to carry me Westward Ho—
To carry me Westward Ho! my boys, that's where the cattle stray
On the far Barcoo, where they eat nardoo, a thousand miles away.

Chorus:
Then give your horses rein across the open plain,
We'll ship our meat both sound and sweet, nor care what some folks say;
And frozen we'll send home the cattle that now roam
On the far Barcoo and the Flinders, too, a thousand miles away.

Knee-deep in grass we've got to pass—for the truth I'm bound to tell—
Where in three weeks the cattle get as fat as they can swell—
As fat as they can swell, my boys; a thousand pounds they weigh,
On the far Barcoo, where they eat nardoo, a thousand miles away.

No Yankee hide e'er grew outside such beef as we can freeze;
No Yankee pastures make such steers as we send o'er the seas—
As we send o'er the seas, my boys, a thousand pounds they weigh—
From the far Barcoo, where they eat nardoo, a thousand miles away.

(Nardoo: a native plant used by Aborigines in the north for food in the form of a flour-like substance.)

The Old Bullock Dray

Oh, the shearing is all over,
    And the wool is coming down,
And I mean to get a wife, boys,
    When I go up to town;
Everything that has two legs
    Represents itself in view,
From the little paddy-melon
    To the bucking kangaroo.

Chorus:
So it's roll up your blankets,
    And let's make a push;
I'll take you up the country,
    And show you the bush;
I'll be bound you won't get
    Such a chance another day,
So come and take possession
    Of my old bullock dray.

Now I've saved up a good cheque,
    I mean to buy a team,
And when I get a wife, boys,
    I'll be all serene;
For, calling at the depot,
    They say there's no delay
To get an off-sider
    For the old bullock dray.

Oh, we'll live like fighting cocks;
    For good living, I'm your man.
We'll have leather jacks, johnny cakes,
    And fritters in the pan;
Or, if you'd like some fish,
    I'll catch you some soon,
For we'll bob for barramundies
    Round the banks of a lagoon.

Oh, yes, of beef and damper
*   I take care we have enough,*
And we'll boil in the bucket
*   Such a whopper of a duff;*
And our friends will dance
*   To the honour of the day,*
To the music of the bells,
*   Around the old bullock dray.*

Oh, we'll have plenty girls,
*   We must mind that.*
There'll be flash little Maggie
*   And buckjumping Pat;*
There'll be Stringybark Joe,
*   And Greenhide Mike.*
Yes, my Colonials, just
*   As many as you like.*

Now we'll stop all immigration,
*   We won't need it any more;*
We'll be having young natives,
*   Twins by the score;*
And I wonder what the devil
*   Jack Robertson would say*
If he saw us promenading
*   Round the old bullock dray.*

Oh, it's time I had an answer,
*   If there's one to be had,*
I wouldn't treat that steer
*   In the body half as bad;*
But he takes as much notice
*   Of me, upon my soul,*
As that old blue stag
*   Off-side in the pole.*

Oh, to tell a lot of lies, you know it is a sin.
*   But I'll go up county*
And marry a black gin.
*   Oh, 'Baal gammon whitefeller,'*
This is what she'll say,
*   'Budgery you*
And your old bullock dray.'

(Paddy Melon: A small wallaby. Jack Robertson: NSW Premier who introduced the Land Bill. Budgery you: Good fellow, you.)

The Dog on the Tucker Box
(Air: 'Camooweal Races')

I'm used to punchin' bullock teams
*   Across the hills and plains,*
I've teamed outback this forty years
*   In blazin' droughts and rains,*
I've lived a heap of troubles down
*   Without a bloomin' lie,*
But I can't forget what happened to me
*   Nine miles from Gundagai.*

'Twas gettin' dark, the team got bogged,
*   The axle snapped in two,*
I lost me matches and me pipe,
*   So what was I to do?*
The rain came on, 'twas bitter cold,
*   And hungry, too was I,*
And the dorg sat in the tucker box
*   Nine miles from Gundagai.*

Some blokes I knows has stacks o' luck
*   No matter 'ow they fall,*
But there was me, Lor' luv a duck,
*   No blessed luck at all.*
I couldn't make a pot o' tea,
*   Nor get me trousers dry,*

And the dorg sat in the tucker box
Nine miles from Gundagai.

I can forgive the blinkin' team,
I can forgive the rain,
I can forgive the dark an' cold,
An' go through it again.
I can forgive me rotten luck,
But hang me till I die,
I can't forgive that plurry dorg,
Nine miles from Gundagai.

('Sat' is obviously a euphemism. This traditional ditty, collected by the Sydney Folklore Society, is sometimes confused with the Jack Moses verse *Nine Miles from Gundagai.*)

The Stockman's Last Bed

Whether stockmen or not,
For a moment give ear—
Poor Jack, he is dead,
And no more shall we hear,
The crack of his whip ,
Or his steed's lively trot,
His clear, 'Go ahead',
*Or his jingling quart-pot**

For he sleeps where the wattles
Their sweet fragrance shed,
And tall gum-trees shadow
The stockman's last bed.

One day, while out yarding,
He was gored by a steer,
'Alas!' cried poor Jack,
'It's all up with me here;
And never shall I

*A cylindrical tin vessel used by bushmen as a kettle; the lid serving as drinking-cup.

The saddle regain,
Or bound like a wallaby
Over the plain.'

So they've laid him where wattles
Their sweet fragrance shed,
And tall gum-trees shadow
The stockman's last bed.

His whip at his side,
His dogs they all mourn;
His horse stands awaiting
His master's return;

While he lies neglected—
Unheeded he dies,
Save Australia's dark children,
None knows where he lies.

For he sleeps where the wattles
Their sweet fragrance shed,
And tall gum-trees shadow
The stockman's last bed.

Then, stockmen, if ever,
On some future day,
While following a mob,
You should happen to stray—
Oh! pause by the spot,
Where poor Jack's bones are laid,
Far, far from the home, where
In childhood he played.

And tread softly where wattles
Their sweet fragrance shed,
And tall gum-trees shadow
The stockman's last bed.

Holy Dan

It was in the Queensland drought,
*   And over hill and dell,*
No grass—the water far apart,
*   All dry and hot as hell.*
The wretched bullock teams drew up
*   Beside a water-hole—*
They'd struggled on through dust and drought,
*   For days to reach this goal.*

And though the water rendered forth,
*   A rank, unholy stench,*
The bullocks and the bullockies
*   Drank deep, their thirst to quench.*

Two of the drivers cursed and swore,
*   As only drivers can.*
The other one, named Daniel,
*   Best known as Holy Dan,*
Admonished them and said it was
*   The Lord's all-wise decree,*
And if they'd only watch and wait,
*   A change they'd quickly see.*

'Twas strange that of Dan's bullocks,
*   Not one had gone aloft,*
But this, he said, was due to prayer
*   And supplication oft.*
At last, one died but Dan was calm,
*   He hardly seemed to care.*
He knelt beside the bullock's corpse,
*   And offered up a prayer.*

'One bullock, Thou hast taken, Lord,
*   And so it seemeth best.*
Thy will be done, but see my need,
*   And spare to me the rest!'*

A month went by. Dan's bullocks now
  Were dying every day,
But still on each occasion would
  The faithful fellow pray,
'Another Thou hast taken, Lord,
  And so it seemeth best.
Thy will be done, but see my need,
  And spare to me the rest!'

And still they camped beside the hole,
  And still it never rained,
And still Dan's bullocks died and died,
  Till only one remained.
Then Dan broke down—good, Holy Dan—
  The man who never swore.
He knelt beside the latest corpse,
  And here's the prayer he bore.

'That's nineteen Thou hast taken, Lord,
  And now you'll plainly see,
You'd better take the bloody lot,
  One's no damn good to me.'
The other riders laughed so much
  They shook the sky around,
The lightning flashed, the thunder roared
  And Holy Dan was drowned

On the Road to Gundagai

Oh! we started down from Roto, when the sheds had all cut out.
We'd whips and whips of Rhino, as we meant to push about;
So we humped our blues serenely, and we made for Sydney Town,
With a three spot cheque between us, as wanted knocking down.

Chorus:
But we camped at Lazy Harry's, on the road to Gundagai,
The road to Gundagai! Not five miles from Gundagai!
Yes, we camped at Lazy Harry's, on the road to Gundagai.

Well, we struck the Murrumbidgee near the Yanko in a week,
And passed through old Narrandera and crossed the Burnet creek;
And we never stopped at Wagga, for we'd Sydney in our eye,
But we camped at Lazy Harry's, on the road to Gundagai.

Chorus: *But we camped, etc.*

Oh! I've seen a lot of girls, my boys, and drunk a lot of beer,
And I've met with some of both, chaps, as has left me mighty queer;
But for beer to knock you sideways, and for girls to make you sigh,
You must camp at Lazy Harry's, on the road to Gundagai.

Chorus: *But we camped, etc.*

Well, we chucked our bloomin' swags off, and we walked into the bar,
And we called for rum-and-raspb'ry and a shilling each cigar;
But the girl that served the pizen, she winked at us so sly,
That we camped at Lazy Harry's, not five miles from Gundagai.

Chorus: *So we camped, etc.*

In a week the spree was over, and the cheque was all knocked down,
So we shouldered our 'Matildas', and we turned our backs on town;
But the girls they stood a nobbler and we sadly said 'Good-bye',
And we tramped from Lazy Harry's, not five miles from Gundagai.

Chorus: *And we tramped from, etc.*

On the Diggings

The Diggers

When first I left old England's shore,
  Such yarns as we were told,
As how folks in Australia
  Could pick up lumps of gold;
So, when we got to Melbourne town,
  We were ready soon to slip
And get even with the captain—
  All hands scuttled from the ship.

We steered our course for Geelong town,
  Then north-west to Ballarat,
Where some of us got mighty thin,
  And some got sleek and fat.
Some tried their luck at Bendigo,
  And some at Fiery Creek;
I made a fortune in a day
  And spent it in a week.

The Old Palmer Song

The wind is fair and free, my boys,
  The wind is fair and free;
The steamer's course is north, my boys,
  And, the Palmer we will see.
And the Palmer we will see, my boys,
  And Cooktown's muddy shore,
Where I've been told there's lots of gold,
  So stay down south no more.

Chorus:
So, blow ye winds, heigho
A digging we will go,
I'll stay no more down south, my boys,
So let the music play.
In spite of what I'm told,
I'm off in search of gold,
And make a push for that new rush
A thousand miles away.

So let us make a move, my boys,
  For that new promised land,
And do the best we can, my boys,
  To lend a helping hand,
To lend a helping hand, my boys,
  Where the soil is rich and new;
In spite of blacks and unknown tracks
  We'll show what we can do.